TAKING

THE

MEDICINE

Simon O'Corra

Characters:

Susan: 34, Black British, Londoner, Clever, Conscious of her Roots, Kind, Excited, Supportive, Caring, Frustrated, Adult, Socialist/Humanist, Techie, Researcher, Mentally Ill Controlled by Drugs.

James: 47, Scottish, Bluff, Sensitive, PTSD, Controlling, Bolshy, Artistic, Chauvinistic, Chip on his Shoulder, Afraid, Addicted,Panicky, Weak, Impatient, Middle aged, Apolitical.

Enid: 67, White from Bristol, Kindhearted, Silly, Romantic, Frenetic, Subservient, Foolish, Pained, Abused, Rejected, Ordinary, Maternalistic, Older, Apolitical, Cheeky, Dreamy, Learning Disabled.

Charlie: 76, White from Somerset, Autistic, Un-socialised, Spoiled, Egotistical, Unaware, Bombastic, Paternalistic, Boastful, Opinionated, Old, Obsessive, Compulsive, Mixed Politics, Deaf, Inflexible.

Caroline: 51, White from Hertfordshire, Snooty, Arrogant, Opinionated , Bigotted, Posh, Gullible, Flippant, Uncaring, Middle Aged, Conservative/Liberal, Rude, Self-Important, Shallow.

Matt: 21 from Manchester, Passive-aggressive, Vulnerable, Double Dealer, Infiltrator, Manipulator, Self-serving, Young, Coalition Politics, Greedy, Stupid, Mean.

Archie: 28, from London, Sharp, Bright, Curious, Steady, Secretive, Kind, Friendly, Policeman, Fraud Expert, Determined.

ACT ONE, SCENE ONE -

Lights up on a messy room little more than a storeroom, with two committee members Enid and Susan already there, Enid prepping her shopping and Susan on her laptop.

ENID: Look I got crisps, biscuits, and cakes, what do you think of this one? Extra Choc-Chip chocolate fudge slab. Iceland are the best! It is so exciting to shop there. *(Enid reaches inside another carrier bag and pulls out, a pack of sausage rolls)*

CAROLINE: Oh, really dear, it might be better to go to the health food store for our nibbles!

ENID: That stuff costs a fortune, anyway it gives you the trots. My old Mum was a stickler for good organic food, but my Dad used to complain about her extravagance. There was a fella that Mum used to read about, oh what was his name? He was high up in organic farming. In her 'sharper' periods she used to bang on about him to Dad.

CAROLINE: Well, good food is, as good food does! Look at me! I am in great shape I am a walking advert for the benefits of organic food, unlike some.

ENID: Oh what was, that man's name? He was a German, I think, so Dad didn't like that either.

CAROLINE: We mustn't be racist Enid. His being German is not important at all.

ENID: I didn't mean anything by it. *(enter Charlie)* Would you like a cuppa Charlie?

CHARLIE: Yes, go on, I don't mind if I do. *(crosses to the food table)* What is this all about? So who are you trying to think of Enid?

CAROLINE: She is trying to remember some organic farming expert. Frankly, I am amazed you know what organic means Enid.

CHARLIE: Oh, Caroline, do leave her alone.

ENID: It's a man my Mum used to talk about, he was an expert on organic food. He was a German I think.

CAROLINE: (*to Charlie*) That makes a difference I suppose , him being a German I mean.

CHARLIE: Oh you must mean Hans Muller and Maria Bigler, they were Swiss actaully, from Emmental.

ENID: I love that cheese, it's the one with holes isn't it.

CHARLIE: What you may not know is that Emmental cheese comes from the Emme Valley. The silly buggers didn't think to protect the name though so now you get Emmental in France and elsewhere.

CAROLINE: I suppose they'll try to get it protected one of these days like Stilton Cheese and Melton Mowbray pies.

CHARLIE: No need because someone canny in Switzerland did get the name and recipe of Emmentaler Switzerland protected.

ENID: Why does it have holes? It seems a waste of money paying for air.

CHARLIE: At the end of the cheese-making process a bacteria *Propionibacterium freudenreichii* consumes the lactic acid excreted by the two other bacterium present, and releases carbon dioxide gas which slowly forms the bubbles that make the holes. It is used in gratins and fondues.

CAROLINE: Yes and it's quite low grade don't you think?

ENID: That is a bit holier than thou. Ha Ha! I know what I like that's all.

CAROLINE: I know it is just my opinion but....

CHARLIE: Anyway as I was saying the Mulllers, the two of them actually married in 1914, developed a natural and sustainable approach to farming, in association with Hans Peter Rusch. That was back in 1946. Did you know I actually used to know someone, Jimmy Baxter, from Arbroath, his Dad was a big industrialist up there, who used to manage an organic market garden back in 1956. He studied organics under Lady Eve Balfour. She was Arthur Balfour's niece.

CAROLINE: See it is as I always say the aristocracy always has the interests of the people at heart. I love to visit Sissinghurst. What Vita Sackville West did for that place! Amazing! Who was he though?

CHARLIE: Arthur Balfour was this country's Prime Minister between 1902 and 1905. My aunt May married a Balfour, they ran a small department store in Prestwich, that's in Manchester you know. You know the sort of thing, a little bit of everything for the discerning customer. They did well until the Arndale Centre opened in the 1970's and then overnight the game was up. They came away with a tidy sum though, they were clever enough to have bought the building when it became available. No leasing for them they played it all by the book and protected their assets. I think the building is now a Restaurant and Nightclub. Oh where was I? To get back to what I was saying: the market garden was all organic, I mean everything, but these days the multi-nationals, the supermarkets and even those high street health shops that peddle the organic stuff are hoodwinking all of us. They just put the same product in different wrappers.

CAROLINE: Oh, don't be so silly Charles. They would never do that and even if they did they could never get away with it.

CHARLIE: You are talking about the Trades Description Act I suppose? Well when you watch exposé documentaries you can see that such things don't work if the multi-nationals have so much money and wield such power? I was reading about GM foods the other day, my goodness it is mad muddle out there. You really have to keep abreast of these issues, I can tell you. If you take your eye off the ball then you are done for. There is even a famous computer tycoon working with a multi national food producer to get control of the world's grain supply. Although what a man who makes PC's has to do with food I'll never know. Can you believe that?

CAROLINE: No not really but...

CHARLIE: Let me finish....I read about this online, and not just from one site, there is a lot of evidence around, particularly from America, where information is all so public. The Americans are unfortunately too reticent to go looking for knowledge most of the time though, which suits the multi-nationals down to the ground.

CAROLINE: I check the labels on everything unlike some (*looking at to Enid)* Can I have a cup of tea, dear, I'm parched. (*crosses to Enid.*)

CHARLIE: (*Facing into the audience*) What you may not realise, is that GM seeds do not regenerate, so farmers have to keep buying new seeds every year and they can only buy those seeds if they agree to buy that particular company's fertilsers too. There are dirty tricks campaigns all around us, it seems that the grain company in question discredits organic farmers. Are you listening to this Caroline? (*looking back at Caroline as she pulls a face and then nods*)They do this by planting GM crops in adjacent fields to organic ones and this means that the organic crops are contaminated. (*pause*) Where do you get your food from again Caroline? Somewhere very special no doubt. Would it be organic by any chance?

CAROLINE: Actually I have a lot of food delivered from France, especially if I am entertaining. I can trust its quality implicitly.

ENID: What can you get from France that you can't get here?

CAROLINE: Well the finest cheeses to start with, Foie Gras of course, truffles and my mushrooms of course.

ENID: I am guessing that Emmental is not among them. Ha! And, Mushrooms, what's wrong with English mushrooms? What happened to all those 'Buy British' campaigns on the telly? I would have thought you being a posh lady, would have been into all that.

CAROLINE: My mushrooms are picked from forests and flown over that same day. They are delicious.

CHARLIE: I assume you have not heard the latest health news from Europe?

CAROLINE: What news is that Charlie? Have you got some more scaremongering for us? I don't believe half the stuff one reads on the internet anyway, but it keeps some silver surfers off the street, only kidding Charles. I do believe though that you get what you pay for and quality will out in the end.

CHARLIE: There is a new strain of tapeworm they have found in Europe. Apparently, the disease is called, oh let me try to remember it… (*pulling out a notebook*) Ah, here it is. I think I wrote it down, oh yes Aveolar Echinococcosis and it is caused by an infection from the larval stage of Echinococcus multilocularis, an exotic tapeworm found in foxes.

CAROLINE: So can that have any impact on we humans?

CHARLIE: Well it seems people get infected by accidentally eating the tapeworm eggs that have passed out in the faeces of infected foxes and dogs

CAROLINE: But Charles you do not think I eat faeces, surely.

CHARLIE: I thought you might mix with those fox hunters who go over to France to beat the ban. You ought to be careful, you know.

CAROLINE: No I do not, I am totally against fox hunting I always have been. Anyway none of my friends eat shit.

ENID: Oooh Caroline how rude!

CHARLIE: The word shit comes from the Old english word Scitte or Diarrhea.

CAROLINE: Does that apply to the verbal kind? (*softly*)

CHARLIE: I am glad to hear it Caroline, but I wasn't implying that you did. Luckily, more people talk shit than eat it. My old teacher Mr Brand could talk for England and most of it was rubbish. What I meant was if you were a huntress, then you might get close enough to a fox to be at risk. Of course even more importantly you can actually get it by eating contaminated mushrooms.

CAROLINE: I have no worries there. The company has strict quality control I have visited their establishment, when I first decided to order the my mushrooms from them, that is why I pay a premium to ensure against such things.

MATT: Hello, everyone, Hi there Enid, Caroline how nice to see you... Am I interrupting, sorry …

CAROLINE: Hello, Matt, how are you. It is lovely to see you. How is the job hunting going? Are you enjoying your time off at present?

MATT: I've some things in the pipeline you know, nothing much yet though.

CAROLINE: Oh, I am sure you will do very well at whatever you turn your hand to.
By the way. How are you finding being on the Management Committee? I am sorry we cannot offer you more salubrious surroundings.

MATT: The last meeting felt like being thrown in at the deep end, I never expected to be taking over as treasurer quite so soon, but I am finding it very interesting, especially at this time in the charity's life when it has so much uncertainty attached to its survival. I hope that I can contribute to saving the group and its services for the future.

CAROLINE: We are a happy band and get things done. We pride ourselves on being welcoming and supportive of each other.

MATT: It is pretty full on, I have quite enough to do with this new job (pointing a huge file at Caroline held in both his hands an putting it down on the table and reaching into his man bag for another one), the paperwork just keeps coming I'm sure there must be an easier way to keep the books.

CHARLIE: I never felt the weight of them myself. It isn't such a big job but it is important to know where the organisation is at any given time. My Dad and me were in business together for years and we always kept our books ship-shape, oh yes!

MATT: The books were sound but I am afraid some of the projections are way off. (*pause)* Times have changed as well, we are able to get away with doing less now as long as the main figures balance up.

SUSAN: Another carb-feast Enid? Is that why we are in such trouble Matt? We never skimp on the refreshments.

ENID: I have to make sure that you all enjoy the food at the meetings. It's my job! It's my JOB and we do have a budget you know, Matt says so. Isn't that right Matt?

MATT: Well............Yes this time Enid *(looking shocked at the carrier bags full of produce*) there are only six of us you know!

ENID: (*emptying yet another bag of goods from a carrier bag*). Well I think because people are giving their time for free so we must make an effort to make them feel appreciated.

CAROLINE: There are limits though Enid dear.

SUSAN: Anyhow we don't need so many carbs Enid. In fact they're not needed at all. Carbs are superfluous. Carbs we can do without. When we eat healthily we produce our own protein and fat.

ENID: Some of us more than others. I just *cannot* shake the fat no matter what I do.

SUSAN: (*opens her laptop and reads out from it*) I was reading a novel last week, The Genesis Secret, it's really grisly mind you, towards the end this professor who knows all about our imposed reliance on carbohydrates gets his rib cage opened up and his lungs ripped out....by this emissary of the Ruling Elite.

ENID: Oh Susan, that's horrible, really don't talk about it.

CAROLINE: Oh, Susan please you're scaring poor Enid and the rest of us for that matter, it all sounds a bit farfetched. It is a novel you say, so we can take all that stuff with a pinch of salt I think. Who are these Ruling elite anyway?

SUSAN: I thought you weren't interested. As I was saying ......this man is a historian who found out that years ago, I mean a long time ago, humans only ate meat until some weird tall men turned up and told them about wheat and stuff, and got them to start growing it and eating it. Thing was, we never needed carbs, it was the first example of being hoodwinked by men in marketing.

CHARLIE: That's sort of the right tack, (*takes out his notebook again and flicks through the pages*) but the real story however is much more interesting. Eleven and half thousand years ago, Emmer was the first kind of crop, a kind of wheat. In 1906, Aaron Aaronsohn re-discovered Wild Emmer wheat growing in Rosh Pina in what is now Israel. It created a real stir. Before that traces of Emmer wheat were only found at ancient sites in tombs. We've come along way to get to GM grains since then, but the original introduction of Emmer was nevertheless a great leap forward in food production. An interesting fact is that the use of grains led directly to a decline in people's teeth and in their stature.

SUSAN: Perhaps that was what the tall men wanted, short men can be so much less trouble in battle HA! (closing the iPad)

CHARLIE: Let me finish! All these grains had toxins within them. Phytic Acid was and is the main culprit still. but those early tribesmen found ways to get rid of it by soaking, sprouting and fermenting the seeds for a long time.

SUSAN: Ah, all down the pub for a beer HA!

CHARLIE: Not as simple as that, Susan.

ENID: Oh,would anyone like a beer? I got some for after the meeting is finished (*Charlie crosses to the food table*)

CHARLIE: Just thinking about that, the acid I mean, my Grandson used to love acid drops, no wonder his teeth rotted away. We'd give him them to shut him up he was a fracticious kid.

ENID: Oh I remember Kinderland Acid Drops. They were delicious. We used to be get them at Ashill if we behaved. Didn't they make aniseed balls? Oh and I think Bulls'eyes. Yummy.

CHARLIE: Where was their factory now? Oh yes I remember Wynnum, in Australia. It is a suburb of Brisbane actually. It is a very sporty place, with loads of clubs, it even boasts an Olympic Swimming medallist, Samantha Riley. I think she was accused of using banned drugs or something. I reckon they had it in for her because she was an aborigine. I think they are still going too.

CAROLINE: Who?

CHARLIE: Kinderland, of course.

CAROLINE: Oh just checking Charles, you got off the point a bit then.

SUSAN: You rewarded your grandson with a poison. They are really disgusting things Charles. Every seaside town in Britain has shops selling the vile stuff.

CHARLIE: (*looking at Enid)* No thanks Enid, Doesn't do to drink on the job. (*pause*) What you may not know is that all the old confectionery is coming back into fashion again.(*pause*) Susan, as I was saying. Grains today are not treated like people used to, so the toxins are everywhere now. We have begun to modify ourselves genetically in relation to the toxins but eleven and a half thousand years is nothing in the life of the earth and of mankind. Did you know that 1% of all people with European descent have Celiac Disease as a result?

ENID: What's that?

SUSAN: It's that thing that Jimmy has, you know his bad stomach.

ENID: Oh yes that's awful, the trots you mean. He is a martyr to his peppermint gum.

CAROLINE (*to Matt*) There she goes again, she is fixated.

SUSAN: So these tall blokes then caused all this trouble when they convinced the smaller people to stop eating meat and turn to wheat and rice.

JAMES: So what are you saying Susan, Kublah Kellogg and Hannibal Hershey just showed up and gave us a ray of bloody sunshine, they were a bad uns, weren't they? (*Charlie exits, for toilet*) Was it something I said Charlie?

ACT ONE, SCENE TWO -

Messy meeting room little more than a storeroom

ENID: (*Still busy sorting stuff out, she is a little slow in everything she does*) Where did Charlie go?

CHARLIE: *(enters*) I'm here. Just a call of nature What were we talking about?

JAMES: We were talking about starting the meeting. I call this meeting to order. (*He pulls out his collection of papers and places them neatly on the desk*) We have a lot of bloody work to get through so let's get cracking. No more slacking and no more talking.

ENID: Sorry James I'm not quite ready yet. Anyone else want a hot drink?(*exits*)

JAMES: No..... Wait. Ok, let's wait for Enid shall we?

CAROLINE: (*to Matt*) It's such shame we can't get Enid to change her shopping habits.

MATT: Well, I keep asking her to curb the spending. She spends a fortune on crap, but her heart is in the right place, I suppose.

CAROLINE: Her heart like ours is in shock from all the rubbish she buys for us all. With the amount she buys, even though it is cheap, she could buy good quality produce just less of it.

MATT: It's so difficult to talk to her about it though, as it's her baby. I don't to rock the boat too early on.

CAROLINE: Don't worry I'll have a word with her. We simply need to sort this out. You can rely on me.

MATT: I'd be very grateful. It would be better coming from you.

ENID: *(enters)* Here I am! Matt, I did well again this week, Iceland had a sale on. I don't know how they do it. Oh and the Pound Shop had a special offer on tea bags and pink custard creams.

MATT: OH.......well done

CAROLINE: (*to Matt*) Leave her to me. Enid dear, we cannot possibly eat 10 packets of biscuits in one meeting, Don't you think 10 packets is a little excessive? How can we six people possibly eat them all today?

ENID: I bought my Mum's old biscuit tin with me this time. We can empty them all into it, those that are left that is. They'll keep fresh. I used to keep all my toiletries in it but I gave it a good wash.

JAMES: That is very good Enid, but can you hurry up please? We must start the meeting and get on with the agenda. Come on hurry up and sit down.

ENID: Just making a tea for myself. I'm waiting for the kettle to boil. Do you want one James?

JAMES: NO! I don't. Thank you.

ENID: A watched kettle never boils, my old Mum used to say Ha! (*hands round biscuits*)

CHARLIE: Enid has a good point there. How do they make it so cheap people say. I hear people all the time saying that, although it never stops them buying BOGOF!

ENID: I hope they're not buying stolen goods, I know I wouldn't.

SUSAN: You mean 'knock offs' Enid. (*pause*) Charlie, some of us have no choice.

CHARLIE: But, food really is an industry now. It is a big business tied into big Government. The Americans are the worst at it. The FOOD and DRUGS AGENCY are a rum lot. They are there to protect the public apparently, but some of the things they are doing beggar belief. Did you know the Food and Drugs Agency in America are trying to outlaw vitamin and mineral supplements, and even homeopathy is coming in for trouble. It is the same in Canada and listen to this: even in The Common Market.

CAROLINE: Surely you mean the European Union?

CHARLIE: It was the Common Market in my day. Anyway, they are now saying that drinking water is not linked to re-hydration. I suppose we all should be drinking those vile fizzy re-hydration drinks now. I remember when Lucozade was given only when someone was ill.

ENID: Oh, yes I remember that when I had my bilious attacks, Mum would give me that. It tasted funny and nice. I was always having bilious attacks.

CAROLINE: No surprise there Enid.

SUSAN: I remember that too. But Charlie, the jury is out on some of the cheaper vitamins and minerals, especially those from the Third World and Eastern Europe. They're not all they're cracked up to be.

CHARLIE: But they are denying the choice of millions to try to look after themselves. I think it's because they want to control the food supply, they want us to buy just what they want to sell. Not a real choice in fact. So many people fall for it because food stuffs are so cheap.

SUSAN: They maybe don't have a choice though, as I said before

CHARLIE: Let me FINISH! . People can choose though. There is plenty of information out there to help people make the right food choices for their health. Just look on your thingy, it will tell you everything you need to know. We all could start growing our own fruit and vegetables

CAROLINE: Here, here Charlie. I have my lovely little herb patio.

SUSAN: I am on the fourteenth floor of a high rise, that means there's no chance of that. I don't even have a balcony. Perhaps you might want to dig up the resident's garden at Middleton Square, Caroline.

CAROLINE: Oh I couldn't do that! I would rather DIE!.

CHARLIE: Now, now ladies. I was just saying that if my old friend could do it in 1956, then anyone can do it. There are allotments these days. There was this programme on the BBC about the upsurge in demand for allotments.

CAROLINE: Oh yes I saw that, it was so sweet, a real sense of community, everyone mixed up together, very touching.

CHARLIE: As I was saying before - Archie, my friend from school was no good at anything there apart from growing mustard and cress, he was always so good at that. Mustard and Cress are very good for you.

CAROLINE: You do not need too much of it either. Did you hear that Enid, less is more.

ENID: Yes, Thats what I mean about Iceland, you get more for less, same thing really. Oh, blow it, I didn't turn the kettle on, silly me. Anyone else want anything?

JAMES: Bloody stupid woman, why can't she just sit down, I have to get a handle on this meeting...........Come on we need to get going soon or the time will go away from us.

CAROLINE: Oh go on then Enid, I'll have a herbal tea, of course. Passiflora and Gentian. Can I have a saucer and a spoon with it. I'll take my own bag out. I must pop to the ladies room, I will return. (*Exits*)

CHARLIE: Me too.

ENID: Hopefully not the ladies room Charlie.

CHARLES: This damn prostate trouble. (*Exit*) It's a nuisance.

ACT ONE, SCENE THREE -

Messy meeting room little more than a storeroom

CHARLIE: (*Enters*) That is better.

JAMES: Damn! Look, I'll be back in a while (*Exits*)

MATT: What's wrong with him?

CAROLINE: (*Enters)*He is in a mood. He can be so grumpy really.

MATT: I hope he's not mad at me.

CAROLINE: Don't be silly you are doing the very best you can dear boy. I dare say the books were in a mess when you took over.

MATT: You're not kidding. Some people just never know when to give up.

CHARLIE: These are lovely. Lemon tarts have always been my favourite. Just a little treat now and again doesn't do any harm

ENID: See I told you. A little of what you fancy my old Dad used to say.

SUSAN: I guess we had better start soon. Where is James?

ENID: All this stuff is delicious. I love it!

CHARLIE: YES! But as I was saying, most of it is full of rubbish. Take Nestle!

ENID: It's Nestles isn't it. When I got a milky bar in Ashill, we always used to sing that song what was it now, (*sings*) '*The*

Milky Bar Kid is strong and tough, only the best is good enough'.....

CHARLIE: Please Enid, do let me finish.

CAROLINE: I prefer Nestlé . It sounds so much more classy.

CHARLIE: As I was saying (*pulls out his little notebook again and flicks through it*) I read recently that Nestlé is about to put in a bid for Hsu Fu Chi, the Chinese biscuit, cake and pudding maker. Can you believe it? There are now 92 million Chinese suffering from diabetes. No wonder I suppose. Did you know that 347 million people have diabetes worldwide and global sales of medication for it top $35 billion every year. My grandad got the kind of diabetes related to getting older though so there is no diabetes in the family. That's why I am able to eat a little sugar now and again. (*taking another two lemon tarts)*

ENID: I got some Ben and Jerry's ice cream for later. (*crosses to fridge*) I suppose that's is full of sugar too.

CHARLIE: The sugar is bad enough but you need to look out for the corn syrup, there was a report last year about Ben and Jerry's, they are owned by Unilever you know. They were very naughty because they put All Natural on their labels but had to drop that after public pressure, It seems that Unilever use mostly unnatural ingredients with only 10% being remotely natural. Did you know that corn syrup can cause a whole range of health problems, like liver and pancreas problems and heart disease, not to mention high insulin levels. See Caroline? The internet does have its uses. My Dad suffered with his liver, he used to produce so much bile, he used to turn quite yellow with it, I was a jaundice baby too, that could be where I got it from.

ENID: I've got a new boyfriend (*Charlie takes 6 biscuits from the table*)

SUSAN: Really? (*closing down her laptop.*)

ENID: Yes, I am on one of those dating sites, they let me use the computer at the Foyer.

CAROLINE: You? YOU are you on a dating site?

SUSAN: Why ever not, Caroline? Romance is open to everyone surely. Hope you're looking after yourself and being careful, I know it is possible to find love online these days, even if some don't agree with people like us having a life.

ENID: He's lovely, you know! He doesn't have a picture mind you, but he's seen mine and he says such nice things about me. I think he loves me. He says nobody understands him, bless him.

SUSAN: Where does he live? What does he do? (*James enters*)

ENID: We've been talking for weeks. I don't know that. He just asks me questions all the time, in between being all mushy and gooey of course. Susan, I really like him. I think he might be the one.

CHARLIE: You want to take care with him he sounds crooked. You don't want to trust to the internet. You don't know who you are talking to. You hear of all these scammers, these crooks. We used to have these door to door salesman coming and calling years ago, you don't see them now, but back then it was a very popular occupation. My old mum used to lock the doors and hide behind the curtain in the front room. She used to say 'you can never be too sure.' (James comes back in)

SUSAN: How long have you been chatting?

JAMES: Bloody ages if her tea making skills are anything to go by!

ENID: We've been going steady for over three months now.

CAROLINE: And you haven't met him yet?

ENID: He respects me and anyway he lives in Cardiff. He' says he will come to see me when he gets some money together.

CHARLIE: There you are what did I say. You have to watch them when they slip in something about money. You watch you do not get scammed. There have been a lot of hoaxers from Africa and Eastern Europe exposed recently. It seems like the current scam is to say you are a business man who has been paid with a cheque that you cannot cash where you are. They offer to send the cheque to you and then get you to cash it and send the proceeds minus a small fee of course back to them via Western Union, of course the cheque bounces and you are left with paying back the cash advance company. So you watch out Enid, don't go sending him your life savings. These people are devious as hell.

SUSAN: So he's WELSH? Why doesn't he have money to come down?

ENID: No he's from abroad I think, he's got a funny accent too. Like those bad guys in the James Bond films, I love them films, my Dad did too, and like Pavel, the cleaner who works in the Foyer.

CAROLINE: So from Eastern Europe? You ought to be careful. They're only out for one thing.

ENID: I've told him that I not prepared to, you know, until we know each other better.

CAROLINE: I meant money, Enid.

CHARLIE: Yes you should. I remember this friend of mine down at Age Concern used to talk about all the old fools who'd been robbed blind by folks online. It is ok to be a silver surfer but we all still need to watch out. His wife was from Poland I think, she came over after the war. I only ever heard good things about her. It does seem nowadays though that the Poles are getting into crime in a big way.

SUSAN: Surely not all Poles are though Charlie. The ones I know are hardworking people just earning a crust, often to send back to families in Poland. There cannot be anything wrong it that surely.

CAROLINE: Well, it is a shame if we let them work here that they don't put money back into the country.

SUSAN: What about all those people who have off shore accounts, avoiding tax?

CAROLINE: Well, they are British people who have been here for a long time.

SUSAN: So that makes it alright?

ENID: My man is an asylum speaker, I think that's what he said.

SUSAN: No Enid. An asylum seeker. Someone fleeing his own country because he is being abused there.

CAROLINE: More likely he is here seeking work, especially since the Communists lost control.

SUSAN: So you don't know what he does and you don't know why he has no money? Erm......

ENID: But he is a lovely man. He tells me how beautiful I am and how he is desperate to meet me, if only he can get the money together. I am so happy. I hope he gets to come down to meet me. We speak in the chat room on the site every time I can access the computer. His camera has broken though so I can't see him and the one on the Foyer's computer is broken too.

CAROLINE: Perhaps that is just as well for him (*aside*)

Charlie exits.

ACT ONE, SCENE FOUR-

Messy meeting room little more than a storeroom.

JAMES: RIGHT! (*Enters, putting away his tablets in his wallet*) OK come on now people let's get down to business, Right! Do we all have our agendas? (*Charlie comes back in*)

MATT: Damn! Where is mine? Oh well, go ahead I can listen.

CAROLINE: You can share mine, here you are.

ENID: Oooh! Very cosy!

JAMES: Welcome everyone. Right! The agenda for the meeting, Number 1. Who is here, erm, can you take the minutes Caroline?

CAROLINE: Oh! Oh, Yes of course. Go ahead, James, sorry.

JAMES: I'd already started actually! .Right. Number 1, those present and apologies

CAROLINE: Just hold on a moment, I cannot find my pen. It must be in my new bag. (puts designer bag on desk, in clear view, takes out articles, including House and Garden)

CHARLIE: Nice bag, Caroline. That must have cost a fair bob or two.

CAROLINE: Yes it's an exclusive, limited edition one, the company is 150 years old this year. They have been supplying the very best quality wares for all that time.

CHARLIE: Did you know they use child labour in the Far East to create these exclusive handbags? Not such an exclusive item after all. Child Labour is rife and used by all manner of so-called exclusive high end retailers. Did you know there are estimated to be 250 million children aged between 5-14 being exploited as child labourers. (*taking out his notebook*) I watched this documentary once and Hugh Cunningham a social historian said that "*Fifty years ago it might have been assumed that, just as child labour had declined in the developed world in the late nineteenth and early twentieth centuries, so it would also, in a trickle-down fashion, in the rest of the world. Its failure to do that, and its re-emergence in the developed world, raise questions about its role in any economy, whether national or global."*

JAMES: When you are ready, you two.

CHARLIE: So you see everyone (*standing up and heading for another lemon tart*) It is easy to think that we as consumers are to blame for child labour, but in fact it is the producers who decide what we will buy and also have control of the means of production which of course they want to do as cheaply as possible to maximise profits.

CAROLINE: Ok ready now, go ahead

JAMES: Number 2, Minutes of Last meeting

CHARLIE: I have something to say about the last meeting

JAMES: Can I just finish the agenda please Charlie, so everyone knows what we have to do today (*Charlie takes more biscuits*) Number 3, Funding Issues. I am sure everyone that the accounts prepared by Matt will reassure us about this.

MATT: Well we all do need to pull in our belts a bit, make some cuts here and there. It's the same everywhere. If we are clever with our budgets we should be fine.

CHARLIE: 'Clever with our budgets'! That's where youth and inexperience can play against organisations. It is good to have been around the block a few times.....

CAROLINE: A few!

CHARLIE: Then you can understand 'boom and bust' and Charity Law.

MATT: We can all bend the rules a bit Charles surely.

CHARLIE: Rules do not bend! Look where that attitude has got us in today's financial world. All this buying bad debt makes me sick. The money markets are such a scramble. My great niece and her husband are hedge-fund managers and I don't mind telling you I don't trust them. They would have the coats from your back.

ENID: What is a hedge fund? I only know about hedges, my dad used to have marvelous privets, he used to carve them into beautiful shapes. He had a stag, now what were the other ones? Oh yes, a fox, that was running, like it was being chased by a pack of hounds, and a cock! He'd spend hours in the garden. .

CAROLINE: I wonder why. (*pause*) Anyway, Matt comes highly recommended, I am sure we can trust him to do the right thing.

CHARLIE: Hedge Funds my dear are a type of investment, not open to you with your savings or any of us in fact, unless Caroline is hiding a nest egg. They are for large institutions, like Universities, some of which have recently lost massive amounts especially when Iceland went bankrupt a while ago.

ENID: They were open this morning.

CHARLIE: No, Enid Iceland the country.

ENID: I didn't know countries could go bankrupt.

CHARLIE: Well, they can. Surprising isn't it. As I was saying, because hedge funds are not for private individuals except very wealthy ones, it means they are not subject to the same regulations. Very risky if you ask me. As for Matt Caroline, we'll see how his performance rates against others.

JAMES: Look, you lot can we please bloody get back to the matters in hand? (*pause*) Number 4, Any other Business.

ENID: Matt? I need the cash back for refreshments.

JAMES: Oh, please give me strength!!!!

ENID: We were talking about money weren't we?

MATT: Erm......

ENID: I have to have the cash Matt. As my old dad used to say 'Money doesn't grow on trees' He said to me just before I was sent away to Ashill "listen my lovely", he said "it's just too difficult what with Mum's troubles and the time and the money it takes to look after you, the home can look after you properly, and that will make Mum feel better. We'll come and see you when we can." They didn't of course, I suppose I was just too much trouble, they didn't love me. I was lucky if I got a card for my birthday. No visits! But you just have to toughen up which is what I did.

JAMES: (*aside*) For fuck's sake.

SUSAN: I am sure they loved you the best they could.

ENID: I suppose so.

CAROLINE: I bet Ashill looked after you well though. Those children's homes were good.

SUSAN: You're kidding, right? Don't you read the newspapers?

CAROLINE: Well, what are the options for parents who cannot cope?

SUSAN: Does that make brutality ok then?

CAROLINE: That's a bit strong Susan.

ENID: Listen, it was no picnic. The place I was sent to, Ashill was grim. There were over two thousand of us. We had to hand in our clothes when we got there and we got some grubby hand me downs. I heard tell that they sold our clothes; anyway I never saw them again even thirty years later when I left there. It was a scary thing, We had villas, as they called them.......

CAROLINE: How *lovely*. Villas sound nice. I have a holiday villa in Italy.

ENID: No they were dormitories, thirty to forty in a room, a hard single bed each and a locker, I had a few little keepsakes I took in with me and by God I made sure I held onto them. No locker was safe. Food time was just as bad, people used to steal each others food, if that is what you could call it. (looking increasingly angry and breathless) Imagine being just six years old and put away for 30 years in what looked like and was actually a prison. (*Enid starts to cry*)

CAROLINE: It must have been nice to have so much time to yourself

SUSAN: You are joking, aren't you?

CAROLINE: What do you mean?

SUSAN: Tell her Enid, what you told me.

ENID: We didn't have much time, we had to work, there was a laundry, cleaning to do and work on the farm for the lads. Non-stop it was. I worked in the kitchen.

CAROLINE: Oh, I see. Like the proverbial a pig in poo (to Matt)

SUSAN: I heard that Caroline.

ENID: The worst thing was the White Tower, that's where the psychiatrists were and where the treatment took place.

JAMES: Can we please get back to the agenda? Focus. Concentrate. Please.

ENID: Anyway Matt can I have my money? I spent all my benefits on the food, we have to have good food for the meetings, it's very important.

MATT: Leave it with me Enid, I'll get it to you by the end of the meeting. Ok?

ENID: I hope you do, I must say. My money is important to me; I need it for my own shopping. My old dad would say "It's only right if it's owed to you, you should get it, never mind having to wait for it"

JAMES: For God's sake you stupid woman let the money go. Matt said he'll deal with it and he will. Bloody hell just shut up about it.

ENID: I only wanted my money. It is owed to me after all (exits, crying.)

SUSAN: Oh, Enid, don't be upset. Enid, wait.... *(exits after Enid)*

(*James fumbles in his bag again for his tablets ,exits*)

CHARLIE: You could have handled that better!

MATT: Don't you start. She'll get her money, just maybe not today. We can't all have what we want when we want it.

CHARLIE: That's cloud cuckoo land. What you need to understand is if the books do not balance they do not balance and no amount of pretending otherwise is going to make a blind bit of difference. Telling the truth is important. Where is the financial report, we needed one before the meeting, and so far there is no sign of one. My old Dad would never keep our business troubles to himself, he always stipulated that we be realistic about what was happening. That saw us through many a hiccup in business.

MATT: Look, we'll talk about it when the meeting starts again, grandpa.

(*Caroline who has been sitting not knowing what to do or where to look, slightly turns her chair away takes out her Homes and Gardens and starts to read*)

CHARLIE: Evasion is never a good way forward Matt.

ACT ONE, SCENE FIVE-

Messy meeting room little more than a storeroom.

MATT: Look just leave it right. OK? Having a go at me won't change the shit we are in. (James enters., Caroline still reading the Homes and Gardens,) It's really not useful old man.

CHARLIE: I am not having a go. I just want to see due process followed. After all the rules are there for a reason, and if rules are bent trouble ensues, then conflicts are set up and you end up on a spiral of deceit.

MATT: I'm not a liar, take that back old man.

SUSAN: Guys! Please. Cool it. Matt I am sure that Charles wasn't implying....

MATT: Well it sounded like it to me

CHARLIE: (*Charlie crosses to the refreshments table to make himself a cup of tea, Enid enters.)* I'm having a warm sugary drink?

SUSAN: Perhaps you'd like one too Enid. Charles can you make Enid a drink?

CHARLIE: Oh, ok.

JAMES: BLOODY BUGGER!

ENID: Thank you Charles, crack open the biscuit barrel too. (*crosses to Caroline*) Caroline did I ever tell you about my story at Ashill?

CAROLINE: No dear I would love to hear about it.

ENID: You would? oh thank you. There was this horrible woman at Ashill, Matron Gollidge, if we did things wrong, even taking more food than was allowed she would slap us on the face, really hard too.

CAROLINE: Surely not. Maybe were you being a bit greedy?

ENID: No I wasn't, the portions were criminal, so bloody small.

CAROLINE: She, that matron of yours would never get away with that now. Though I dare say some Mums and Dads would like the option these days.

CHARLIE: I'm with the pro-smacking lobby myself. It never did me any harm. My old Mum only had to raise her voice more than usual and I knew I was in for trouble if I didn't stop doing what I was doing. She only smacked me once when I was about two, after that she said that if I did something that might embarrass myself out in public, I'd know what would happen to me. It worked but it needed one good hiding to make me learn.

ENID: Early on in my stay we had some lessons, Mister Hoggett, or Johnny Hoggett as we called him, he was a tartar. You see the drugs I was on for my fits used to make me quite slow and a bit clumsy and sometimes I'd make a mark on my page with the pen. it leaked ink you know.

CAROLINE: Oh a pen, like mine. They're called 'fountain pens'.

ENID: Mine was more of a waterfall than a fountain. Ha ha! Yes that's it. Anyway he saw what I'd done and he said to me if I did it again I'd get a wallop, and do you know next time he hit me on the head with my chalk board. It bloody hurt I can tell you. He said he'd knock some sense in.

CAROLINE: That's awful Enid. I am sorry. It must have been an awful time at Ashill, did you ever stay anywhere else? What about work? Did you do any work?

ENID: Oh yes. After Ashill I was moved to Clifden Hostel, where we did housework for our keep. It was hard work but it got me a job outside a couple of times a week working in a school. I worked in the canteen as a scullery worker, basic stuff but I got my dinner thrown in.

CAROLINE: That must have been a bonus.

ENID: Oh yes it was. The food was damn good. I used to get second helpings.

CAROLINE: Nothing has changed their dear has it?

ENID: Oh I like my food!

Caroline: I can see that......

SUSAN: (talking to Matt) You need to understand that Charles is old school and quite rightly is suspicious about anything that isn't done by the book.

MATT: I know that but it's not like I'm a corrupt MP or anything is it?

SUSAN: It's all relative though Matt, you must see that.

MATT: Anyway they weren't that bad were they? The expenses system exists anyway. So they were using the system.

SUSAN: And how! There are rules like we have here and they are meant to be adhered to, not deviated from. Those MP's used the system to defraud Parliament and more importantly the Public.

CHARLIE: Matt, this is exactly what I am talking about in relation to our group. There is of course a system of expenses for MP's like there is a system for charity financial accounts. I don't have a problem with that per se but these things are so open to misinterpretation and fraud. It is a shame to say but human nature being what it is this cheating the system is prevalent all over. This is exactly why everything relating to systems should be black and white and adhered to so exactly.

MATT: It's not how the world works anymore gramps. I think MP's work damned hard and don't get paid very much in comparison to others. We can't begrudge them a few bonuses.

SUSAN: So being a current MP and making a show of yourself on a reality TV show is a good way of spending tax payers money?

MATT: But that's such fun to see those people make arses of themselves. It makes them human, approachable and is good for ratings.

SUSAN: MP's are supposed to take serious decisions about how this country works, not crawl around on all fours with voluptuous ex-actresses. Daft old bugger.

CHARLIE: They all are, the amount of scandal these people bring on us all, and that's not to mention the celebrities, so-called, who disport themselves all over those dreadful magazines that everyone seems to be reading these days. Well, James? And, are you going to get the meeting back on track? We haven't discussed a thing yet!

JAMES: WHAT! 'WE' haven't discussed a thing yet! Am I hearing you right Charlie?

CHARLIE: I rest my case.

JAMES: I give up.

SUSAN: Are you alright, James?

JAMES: (*reaching for his briefcase and for his tablets*) I'll be ok in a minute.

ENID: What are your pills for James?

JAMES: Oh nothing.

SUSAN: Are you sure you are ok?

JAMES: Yes. YES!! Stop bloody fussing woman.

SUSAN: OK. ok.

JAMES: I just need five minutes, just leave me be.

ENID: I'm not sure that pills often help. (*Looking across at James popping another pill*) I just wanted someone to talk to, someone to sit with me when I was lonely and lost at Ashill. The nights were always the worst. It always seemed that pills were the easier option. They'd make a big show of making you feel special though as they handed those damn silly plastic cups to you and wait just a moment to make sure you swallowed the pills.

SUSAN: It's different now all the online pharmacies make you feel worthless in order to peddle their wares. You can't sleep, then take a pill, you can't wake up then drink this energy drink, eat this burger, take the indigestion pill, fill yourself full of coffee just to keep awake, get home have a ready meal, all those e-numbers mean you cannot sleep, back to square one. If you carry on for a few days then you feel depressed or maybe just stressed and then you turn to the online pharmacies for the panacea of the modern woman or man (directed at James) anti-depressants, they start you off thinking you may just be a little sad so just take the first level......... and so it goes on.

CAROLINE: You wouldn't catch me buying anti-depressants online, I just stick to my laxatives, that's as dangerous as I get.

ENID: Yeah, laxatives with all those dodgy mushrooms must be very dangerous

JAMES: Oh, for fuck's sake....

SUSAN: Let's have a cup of tea shall we?

CHARLIE: Oh yes please I am a bit dry for some reason! (*All move to refreshments)*

ACT ONE, SCENE SIX -

Messy meeting room little more than a storeroom.

ENID: Do you know, I don't know anyone who doesn't take tablets for something. You do don't you? (at James) My doctor seems to keep prescribing more and more stuff. I need stuff for my diabetes and my cholesterol.

CAROLINE: Enid dear, you have diabetes? She eats all that crap no wonder. (*aside*) You know, just because you have the medication doesn't mean you shouldn't change your diet. Every little helps.

SUSAN: I read somewhere that diabetes can be cured with Vitamin D.

CAROLINE: Oh, don't be silly dear, that's impossible. I am sure the doctors know what they are talking about.

CHARLIE: Oh you think so Caroline? I read somewhere, now where was that? Oh, yes I know. It was online somewhere, on a health ranger website. There was a case in the US where a Big Pharma company colluded with a pharmacy consultants which provided medicines for a number of care homes, the consultancy started peddling just those medications produced by the Big Pharma.

ENID: I used to know this man Henry Gunhouse, he was a big farmer. He must have been about 28 stone. Strong as an ox he was, he had a bit of an eye for the ladies too. My Mum included, she used to get free eggs from him. Turns out he wasn't organic though, he got into trouble for using too much of them pesticides, and some of the chemicals got into the water. It was a scandal. My mum was horrified about it. They say he tried to hang himself in his barn, but he weighed so much (patting her thighs) that the king beam busted under his weight. You should have seen his neck, black and blue it was.

The farm was closed down but I don't know what happened to him after that.

CAROLINE: Enid. Charles was not talking about Farmers! Silly woman. He was talking about large pharmaceutical companies. (*pause*) Charlie that example is not about a doctor though.

CHARLIE: Yes but it shows that whatever a doctor prescribes can be manipulated to fit the needs of the providers. There is no monitoring at either end of the healing spectrum.

CAROLINE: Yes ok, but let's keep on the subject. Charlie what tablets do you take?

CHARLIE: I have drugs for my arthritis too, prescribed by a doctor, not sure they do that much good though, but they keep the pharmaceutical companies in business. Who else has tablets here? If you don't mind my asking? What about you Matt?

MATT: Well, I'd rather not say.

ENID: Oh, go on Matt, I told everyone about my drugs.

MATT: I have allergies, and I have an inhaler for my asthma and steroid cream for my eczema. My doctor is very good he makes sure I have what I need.

ENID: It is good when you have a nice doctor. The ones at Ashill were devils, they made me have Electric Shock treatment. I wasn't asked they just came and got me one day and said I had to have some new treatment. I thought it would be some medicine to take or an injection, but looking back I never was taken away before for those. So I was taken into a room and three nurses helped me lie down, and fastened me to the bed, I couldn't argue because I didn't know what was coming up next. The doctor then put these caliper things with pads on my head and the next minute it all went black and the pain was so awful, I passed out I think and when I woke up, I had the worst headache ever.

MATT: Did your hair stand on end? We did this thing at school in Physics where we got to touch this silver dome thing and all our hair stood on end.

SUSAN: It's nothing like that Matt, no comparison at all.

CHARLIE: They're still peddling drugs for the Big Pharmas though

CAROLINE: Doctors you mean?

SUSAN: I take drugs for my condition, my consultant prescribes them, mind you I take more drugs to counter the effects of the first drugs than those drugs themselves. It's scary how many things I take to combat side effects (*shaking her hands in an exaggerated way*) So Caroline what about you?Are you a druggie?

ENID: Oh Susan, that's not nice, I am sure Caroline wouldn't be involved in that. It isn't legal so Caroline wouldn't do it.

CAROLINE: Absolutely not!

SUSAN: No, Enid I meant medicine's not narcotics. I know Caroline isn't that sort of woman. So, Caroline how about it? What medicines do you take?

CAROLINE: Well I take painkillers sometimes for my aches and as I said before something for my, you know….. loo problems. I get my medicine online though, it's much easier and cheaper.

SUSAN: So no prescriptions?

CHARLIE: You can get anything you want at the supermarket villages now. An old friend, Gerald, used to work for one of the big ones, and he used to say it was possible to get practically anything you wanted at the supermarket pharmacy or even in the aisles, a lot of the time.

ENID: What about you James? James? What kind of tablets do YOU take?

SUSAN: Leave him alone Enid. He is resting can't you see?

JAMES: It is ok. I am taking some anti-depressants. They just help to calm me down

CAROLINE: Do they? (*aside*)

MATT: It is hard, Caroline, to keep an organisation on track, sometimes it can be too much for one man to handle.

CAROLINE: I was only saying, I didn't mean anything by it.

MATT: Are you seeing someone for your trouble, James? It might be worthwhile getting yourself sorted out before it's too late.

JAMES: Oh no, I am ok, I just went online and found a great site in the US who helps people with depression,

CHARLIE: What is the site called? I have seen a few online when I have been researching other things. The sites always seem to pop up even if you haven't looked for medications.

JAMES: www.havingasadday.com. They help you get to the bottom of your problem, they have great questionnaires and you can even talk to a real online psychologist in a kind of chat room.

CHARLIE: So www.havingasadday.com. What about having some free counselling or just pulling yourself together? Are those options peddled by this site?

JAMES: I don't want any of that bloody talking therapy. Never gets you anywhere. Action is what is needed. Anyway it's a great site and the medicines are doing me some good now.

CHARLIE: What do you mean, 'now'? It sounds as though things were not always good, I have heard that a lot from forums on websites.

JAMES: Well to start with the tablets made me feel even worse, so I stopped them, but the company very kindly followed up when I didn't buy more and it turns out I am treatment resistant so now they have recommended an extra pill to stop the resistance. They are really very thorough. They kept me from going mad.

CHARLIE: That's one way of looking at it. But if you think about....

SUSAN: I am sorry to hear you have troubles James. I am sure I speak for everyone when I say I hope they continue to work for you. Depression is awful truly it is.

ENID: So there you are - we are all taking tablets.

CHARLIE: And how many of these drugs do we really need? (*taking out his notebook again*) Now evidence is coming to light that suggests many research projects advocating the efficacy of certain drugs have been falsified by health and medical professionals in the research field, many of who work for large Pharma companies. If Big Pharma companies pay for research, how can they be trusted to be impartial when asking people to choose which treatment to use? And another thing.... the advertising strategies that these companies use are despicable.

CAROLINE: Oh here we go again.

CHARLIE: This is serious, let me finish please.....Right as I was saying ......I saw a documentary about advertising and the Big Pharma. This 'Big Pharma' company called Abbotts Laboratories have an advert that depicts a man pressurising his brother to use a statin drug, Niaspan, whilst the advert later goes on to detail the terrible and even lethal side-effects of the drug. This man is seen to be blackmailing his brother by implying that his refusal to take medicine is like being an alcoholic or a drug user.

ENID: It seems we are all drug users HA!

CAROLINE: Well I am actually partial to a bottle of St Emilion, now and again. It is good for the bad cholesterol after all.

CHARLIE: It is serious you know. The brother's family are seen to be negatively judging him if he does not agree to the family and the doctor's demand. There is such peer pressure for everyone to avoid death by taking drugs.

CAROLINE: No one wants to die or lose a loved one.

ENID: I have sometimes wanted to die....

SUSAN: Me too. Anyone else?

CHARLIE: But listen there are so many more things one can try to get well with, rather than just drugs. Talking is a great healer.

JAMES: You know Charlie you may have a point there, but sometimes talking can make things worse. (*reaching inside his briefcase for his tablets again*) Enid lets have a refreshment break shall we.......(*James exits*)

ENID: Oh great! That's ME! (*crosses to table*)

CHARLIE: I second that. I would love a cup of tea.

(*The group disperses again for tea, loo breaks, medication breaks etc)*

ACT ONE, SCENE SEVEN -

Messy meeting room little more than a storeroom.

(*The group reconvenes and everyone has something to eat and drink and generally talks inanities, James sits down and looks defeated, he remains silent for some time*)

JAMES: Look everyone, I can't see us getting any work done, so let's just agree a date for another meeting and give us all some time to have a think about the issues raised by the agenda. I would like us all to think about solutions for our funding issue in time for the next meeting.

MATT: That's great James, we all need to think clearly about a way forward.

CHARLIE: I hope we don't miss the boat with our funding strategy. It would be so easy to fall behind and for it all to be too late. It is good keep an eye on the ball.

CAROLINE: It really is a shame that we cannot at least sort something out now.

ENID: I don't know why we haven't sorted it. In my management committee training last year it said you should always make sure that the meeting does what it says it is going to do right from the start. That's why we have an agenda, isn't it James?

CHARLIE: I agree. We needed reining in, and then we could have done what we set out to. Someone must always take control. Now we will just have to wait until next time

JAMES: If everyone would just bloody stop talking then we might get down to sorting this mess out, but no, on and on the talking goes. So let's agree a time for another meeting and use the rest of this meeting to air all our petty concerns and revolutionary zeal *(Enid crosses to the refreshment table.)* Enid sit down, Please!

ENID: Ok *(walks back to the table)* Ooooh! I like your diary Caroline.

CAROLINE: Oh this! Yes its from Liberty's. They are darling aren't they?

JAMES: Caroline, please. Now how about the same date next month?

CAROLINE: Oh sorry I can't do next month at all, it's Ascot Week and I promised Mummy I would go this year and that is also when I lunch with friends who visit from abroad.

ENID AND SUSAN: I can do it anytime you like.

JAMES: Thank you both for being so flexible. How about you Matt?

MATT: Well I have to keep next month free as I have job interviews and the possibility of a freelance contract with a company July would be better

CAROLINE: Yes for me too

JAMES: Are you sure it is not the Henley Regatta or Badminton?

CAROLINE: James, neither of those take place in June. Nor the Trooping of the Colour as I am sure you know - being an army man.

JAMES: So you could grace us with your presence? Charlie what about you?

CHARLIE: I am sorry to be a killjoy but I have my steam train convention to organise and run in June I can never do anything then. Did I tell you all about my involvement with the Chuffers Society? My best friend Roger Casement from a little village in Somerset, had an uncle who used to drive a steam train. Of course Beeching put paid to that branch line in the 1960's, so the rolling stock was left abandoned and rusting. Roger's Dad was a real enthusiast and a stickler for civic activities so he got the community involved and they re-opened the stretch of line between them and their neighbouring village. Roger's Dad, David Casement, became a local councillor and was well thought of in the community. He did a lot of work for people there. They used a special paint on those steam trains, a sort of plastic polymer mixture guaranteed for 60 years. I did the painting with Roger and few others of course. You can still get that paint if you know where to ask.

CAROLINE: It does not sound very eco-friendly Charles.

JAMES: Let's leave that for later, shall we Charlie. So everyone can we agree the 5th of July, at least we can beat the Olympics Rush.

CHARLIE: If we talk about the Olympics we could be here forever talking about that debacle. I can make that date James.

EVERYONE ELSE: AGREED!

ENID: Can I bring out the refreshments now before we chat?

JAMES: Yes Enid.

(Group breaks up for loo breaks and tablet breaks, Enid finally heads to the refreshments table and starts to unpack the food)

ACT ONE, SCENE EIGHT -

Messy meeting room little more than a storeroom.

ENID: Look at all these goodies everyone......

CAROLINE: Oh save us Enid. We cannot possibly eat all that. And why would we want to?

CHARLIE: It's FAR too much, really it is Enid, but .....just this once. Mmmm Pork pie.

SUSAN: Really Charlie you bang on about all the food piracy in the world then tuck into 'shite'

ENID: And he doesn't even leave any pork pie for anyone else, honestly! (*talking to Susan*) What has he done to deserve that? He just shot his mouth off all day

CHARLIE: Well just because I can talk about what is happening with global food production doesn't mean I cannot take pleasure in some of the rubbish. If not this food then something else will get me before long.....

ENID: OH, that's morbid talk Charlie

SUSAN: Fair point I guess, freedom of choice and all that. But.....When you know what is in our food these days it is sobering to consider what kind of madness is at play. I am amazed that MSG is still allowed in our food. We have known about it for years. (*opening her laptop.*)

ENID: What is MSG?

SUSAN: Mono-Sodium Glutamate or MSG is described as a food additive and flavour enhancer. It is popular in Chinese food

ENID: I *LOVE* Chinese food. I do love a Spring Roll.

CAROLINE: Quelle surprise! How do you know all this stuff Susan?

SUSAN: It is a module on my OU course. The funny thing is, the industry that produces it, says it is a naturally occurring amino acid, but it then states it frees MSG from protein. And! that's not all it is true to say that protein does not contain sodium. So it must be a product and is being mis-labelled. Therefore MSG is a 'product' and not naturally occurring at all. This is supplemented by the fact that MSG is 'patented' so cannot be naturally occurring.

CAROLINE: I thought that it was outlawed a while ago or at least certain producers stopped using it. It gives one the shakes doesn't it.

SUSAN: That's what they want you to believe. They now hide the MSG under a different name so you and I are fooled into believing that MSG has gone.

CAROLINE: So what is called now? I suppose you know?

SUSAN: Glutamic Acid mostly, although this is just one of 25 + ways that MSG is hidden on labeling.

CAROLINE: You do know your stuff don't you? Did you find it hard to get on your course, is it a special one for, well, you know, ...erm....special.

SUSAN: No, not special, they do take Black people on the courses now.

CARLOLINE: Oh, no dear, I didn't mean that.

SUSAN: (*pause*) So anyway, as I was saying MSG can be linked to high blood pressure, adrenal malfunction, diabetes, epilepsy and I think obesity. There is also some evidence of it being addictive or at least making food taste more desirable a fairly compelling reason for manufacturers to use it.

ENID: Yes and another thing a lot of my friends at Ashill and other places were sterilised and they didn't have freedom of choice , terrible it was for them just being told they had to have an operation and bingo, no more kiddies for them.

CAROLINE: Some would say that's for the best Enid

JAMES: For Christ's sake Caroline!

ENID: Would *you* have liked it?

CAROLINE: Well no but....

ENID: Everyone has the right to have a bairn.

CHARLIE: So it seems, which is the pity.

SUSAN: But getting back to the food issue we were talking about...In the US there has been a new Government Act introduced laughingly called, The Personal Responsibility in Food Consumption Act or 'The CheeseBurger Bill' . This would make it illegal to bring law suits against food manufacturers, sellers and distributors. Can you believe it?

CAROLINE: But if that happens we may as well do away with food control and labeling altogether.

SUSAN: Exactly. I cannot believe the Yanks are just gonna lie down and take it.

CHARLIE: That's what Harold Pinter says they are doing right now, and it is killing the world as a result.

ENID: I love Cheeseburgers too. They are so tasty I can't get enough of them.

CAROLINE: I'd never eat a burger at those places, I make my own actually. I must admit though I do love those delicious milk shakes you can get, you know the ones at the fast food places. They are too divine and they are my guilty secret.

SUSAN: That's the intention. But do you know what is in those shakes Caroline? (*reaching for her laptop*) It is here somewhere hold on. Argh here it is. A list of ingredients in a certain High Street Strawberry Milk Shake. amyl acetate, amyl butyrate, amyl valerate, anethol, anisyl formate, benzyl acetate, benzyl isobutyrate, butyric acid, cinnamyl isobutyrate, cinnamyl valerate, cognac essential oil, diacetyl, dipropyl ketone, ethyl acetate, ethyl amyl ketone, ethyl butyrate, ethyl cinnamate, ethyl heptanoate, ethyl heptylate, ethyl lactate, ethyl methylphenyl-glycidate, ethyl nitrate, ethyl propionate, ethyl valerate, heliotropin, hydroxyphenyl-2-butanone, a-ionone, isobutyl anthranilate, isobutyl butyrate, lemon essential oil, maltol, 4-methylacetophenone, methyl anthranilate, methyl benzoate, methyl cinnamate, methyl heptine carbonate, methyl naphthyl ketone, methyl salicylate, mint essential oil, neroli essential oil, nerolin, neryl isobutyrate, orris butter, phenethyl alcohol, rose, run ether, y-undercalctone, vanillin and solvent.

CAROLINE: My God! What are all those things? What do they do to you? I thought it was just ice cream, milk and strawberries, it tastes so realistic.

SUSAN: That's not all, look here..... milk fat and nonfat milk, sugar, sweet whey, high fructose corn syrup, corn syrup, natural and artificial vanilla flavour, guar gum, mono and diglycerides, cellulose gum, sodium phosphate, carrageenan and natural flavours from plant sources

CAROLINE: There are natural flavours though that ought to count for something. Natural means just that doesn't it?

SUSAN: Well......

JAMES: FOR FUCK'S SAKE!!!! You people make me sick. (*stands*) I have never known such a set of self absorbed bastards. Call yourselves caring people? I pity this charity and seriously doubt its chances of survival if all you can talk about is bloody Food, Medicines and sodding handbags and diaries.

MATT: That's a bit harsh James.

JAMES: You can get off your fucking mobile as well. Be fucking present for once. You are supposed to have the financial interests of this charity at the top of your list but look at you. No chance this charity has any hope of surviving with you lot at the helm.

CHARLIE: But YOU are supposed to lead us James. You're the Chair!

JAMES: I would if I could get a fucking word in Charlie!

ENID: That IS true..... you really can talk., Charlie

JAMES: ....and as for you Enid, sorry love but these meetings are not an opportunity to reminisce or gorge ourselves (*takes a large pasty*), oh these pasties are shite, .Oh Beeches. I might have known!!!

ENID: I love Beeches, they are traditional Cornish Pasties

JAMES: My arse they are.

CHARLIE: Did you know it is now illegal to call a pasty 'Cornish' unless it was made in Cornwall? It is a directive from Brussels or Strasbourg. For a pasty to be called 'Cornish' it has to be made in Cornwall and to a certain recipe.

Unfortunately, Beeches fulfill this criteria, you are right though James it doesn't make them taste any better though.

JAMES: Charlie, shut the fuck up! Sorry but we have no more time for this right now.

CAROLINE: James leave Enid alone you can't get what you want by bullying.

JAMES: So how else am I supposed to? It would help if you would stop mooning around and burying your damn head in Homes and Gardens

CAROLINE: Well, really! I try my best, I really do and what do I get.

SUSAN: Where is all this coming from James? What's wrong with you? I know the meeting hasn't really got off the ground but honestly to turn on people like that is out of order

JAMES: Who the hell do you think you are? Fucki.......

(James gasps for breath suddenly and falls to the floor)

SUSAN AND ENID: James!

(Both rushing to his aid, Matt and Caroline dive into their bags and get their mobiles out but there is no signal)

SUSAN: Go on!! Go and find a phone, there is one upstairs. (*Charlie gets up, crosses to the door, and flops into a chair*) What are you doing you old fool?

CHARLIE: There is no point; the phone like everything else, in this place is buggered.

ENID: The kettle's still working. We could have a nice cup of tea.......

BLACKOUT

ACT TWO, SCENE ONE -

New meeting room the ex-theatre space in the community centre.

(*The place is full of rubbish, the old community centre sign covered in riot inflamed profanities. James enters and sorts out papers for all of the people, he lays out water on the table, organises a flipchart and writes up a set of ground rules*)

JAMES: Right, you buggers this time we are going to get some work done. (*sneaks another tablet from his bag.)*

SUSAN: (*enters*) Hello James .How are you feeling?

CAROLINE: (*enters*) ERM....hello all.

MATT: (*enters confidently*) Hi everyone. OK?

CAROLINE: How do you do?

SUSAN: This is even worse than that storeroom we used last time. Let's hope today's meeting doesn't turn into a farce.

CHARLIE: (*enters*) Good day. I hope we have some good news this time, Matt.

MATT: Did you print off my financial projections?

CAROLINE: Yes I did, but maybe next time you could give me more notice?

MATT: I only finalised them yesterday after receiving some startling news about our future.

SUSAN: (*Enid enters*) Hi Enid, how are you doing?

ENID: I am ok .Let me sort all these bags and things out.

SUSAN: Come on tell me what's up.

ENID: (*starting to cry*) I've had such trouble,Susan. That man I told you about the one who was in love with me, well he turned out to be a bad man, he promised me all sorts of things, I thought I could trust him, he seemed so nice online, I'm so sad, I thought we had something going....he 's like all the other people I get close too.... they always hurt me.

CHARLIE: Well it sounds like you had a lucky escape. You cannot trust those Eastern Europeans and you get what you ask for if you use the internet for romance.

SUSAN: Charlie please. Give it a rest. Can't you see she is upset?

CAROLINE: I agree with Charles, Enid, a lucky escape, at least he didn't get any money out of you. You are better off without him.

ENID: I've been such a fool, he promised it was just to help him out and to enable us to be together for a while (sobbing now)

SUSAN: What did you do?

ENID: I sent him some money.

CAROLINE: That was very foolish.

ENID: Now he has disappeared

SUSAN: Bastard!

ENID: That's all my savings gone

CHARLIE: How much?

ENID: £500 .He hurt me, he said he would come over that weekend and that we could be together

CHARLIE: You fool! I told you last time not to give him any money.

ENID: I know Charlie, I've been taken for a ride. And, on top of it all, now we have to work in this dump. I remember when this space was busy every weekend, I used to be in the shows here, we used to make our own costumes and everything. Then there was the karaoke nights I organised for the Gateway Club, I loved that, it was a good laugh.

SUSAN: Look at it now. Sad really, things change I suppose. Those riots last year didn't help, they took the soul out of the area. I bet you were good Enid.

ENID: I was quite the star!

JAMES: So hello everyone....

ALL: Hello James

JAMES: Enid love, why don't you organise some drinks and snacks for us? I just want to say I am sorry about last time, I am a grumpy bugger sometimes.

ENID: Of course James, I am glad to see you looking better.

JAMES: I thought we could have drinks and a chat first , get that out of the way then get on with the important business of the day .

MATT: With regard to that important business I believe I have found a solution for us.

CHARLIE: We ought to wait until the chair has taken us through the agenda

MATT: Yes I know THAT.

JAMES: How are the refreshments coming along?

ENID: Won't be long. A slice of Battenburg anyone?

CAROLINE: I think I'll powder my nose back in a mo.... (*starts to leave then stops*)

MATT: I have a company interested in funding us

SUSAN: Really????

CAROLINE: It is really good news don't you think Susan? They are a pharmaceutical company too.

CHARLIE: What!? I cannot believe that you would consider that after all the debates we had last time about Big Pharma

CAROLINE: Hardly debates (*aside to Matt, laughing*)

CHARLIE: It isn't funny Caroline.

ENID: Well I think if a company want to save our little group then I'm all for it. I want to keep us going for as long as possible. Well done Matt and Caroline

CAROLINE: It wasn't me, it was our young whizz kid.

CHARLIE: But it could be a conflict of interest issue to take the assistance of a pharmaceutical company. Do you know what that is, Enid?

ENID: What's that?

CHARLIE: Well for instance Enid, you are a service user are you not.

ENID: Yes I am.

CHARLIE: So if a service user votes to take the pharmaceuticals money to keep getting their service, some might think that that is a conflict of interest when perhaps we should be trying to get funding from somewhere that isn't directly involved in mental health at all. We cannot take money from just anywhere just because we want the service to continue, we have to think about it. We all have a responsibility to our service users and to the Charity Commission.

ENID: Oh yeah I see....I think...

JAMES: If you'll excuse me. I'll be back shortly; carry on won't you. (*Exits*)

ACT TWO, SCENE TWO -

New meeting room the ex-theatre space in the community centre.

Everyone present.

MATT: I think this is a great opportunity.

CAROLINE: As do I.

ENID: Well if it means the charity is safe it must be good right?

SUSAN: I think we need to consider the wider picture (*getting out her laptop*)

CAROLINE: David Cameron says that the wider picture has been a problem in the past, so his Big Society view is one which does away with centralised government and focusses on local need and autonomy. So there is no reason why we cannot, in order to save ourselves from closure, accept funding from a multi-national corporation.

SUSAN: I have no argument with that theory but the practice is rife with problems and even disaster.

CAROLINE: That is a bit dramatic Susan. Why are you always so negative?

CHARLIE: When I pointed out the dodgy mushrooms story or when Enid corrected your misplaced rose-tinted view of the asylum system, You didn't say that. It is morally lazy not to think through difficult situations.

CAROLINE: How dare you? I take this work on the committee very seriously. I put in the hours and read what I need to know.

SUSAN: But that's just information from lover boy. If you don't look further than your own nose you'll be caught out and eventually led by it.

CAROLINE: What are you saying? What do you mean?

SUSAN: I mean just because you like someone it doesn't mean you have to just take what they say as gospel truth.

CAROLINE: I do listen to Matt, yes, but I also make enquiries of my own.

SUSAN: And, you didn't find out any of the damaging information we did.

MATT: Look Susan what is your problem, I think you have a personal downer on me. It's not very professional now is it?

CAROLINE: What could you expect though from.... *(aside to Matt)*

SUSAN: From? Is that all you both can say? It seems neither of you want to know any other point of view, and I am left wondering why?

MATT: Well we have nothing to hide, go ahead tell us what you know, although all that online stuff can be deceptive

CAROLINE: Let's face it the Open University is not a real University, anyway.

CHARLIE: That is so snobbish. No one has a right to judge another's choice of University.

SUSAN: Well, Fuzzy is one of the pharmaceutical organisations collaborating with the Food and Drugs Agency or FDA and the Codex Alimentaris. This Codex Alimentaris is a body established by the World Health Organisation in the

1960's to monitor food and drug production and to set up standards for these two things. What they are all doing now is systematically attempting to outlaw vitamin and mineral supplements and to forbid any but the lowest dosage in homeopathic medicines.

ENID: I used to have a Kodex camera (*busy with food again*)

CAROLINE: Oh Enid, you silly woman, do shut up. We weren't talking about cameras. How can you expect to make a decision like the one we must make today, if you can't keep up with the discussion. It is probably best if you just let us decide for you. Matt has gone into this in detail.

MATT: Yes, thanks Caroline (*to Charlie and Susan*) Competition is good surely and the allopathic industry does have much greater success than the naturopathic, even you said earlier that Charlie's view that all vitamin and mineral supplements are not good quality.

CHARLIE: In a recent World Health Organisation study, it was revealed that 82% of the world's population uses alternative medicine. That destroys your argument I think Matt.

SUSAN: And, as Charlie said where is the choice if one type of healing has powerful backers at government agency level. This Codex can even impose its dictates in the US thereby countermanding the US constitution, it has that much power.

MATT: I still don't see how this impacts on our getting into bed, as you put it, with FUZZY. Business is business and nothing comes from free anymore.

CHARLIE: Poor old Bevan would be spinning in his grave to hear you say that.

MATT: Who is that? Sounds like an old dog or is it another one of your relations of Prime Ministers I suppose.

CHARLIE: The youth of today are so ignorant. I give up I really do. Anuerin Bevan was instrumental in setting up the National Health Service. He never envisaged private sector involvement in the public welfare sector. He once said "The National Health service and the Welfare State have come to be used as interchangeable terms, and in the mouths of some people as terms of reproach. Why this is so it is not difficult to understand, if you view everything from the angle of a strictly individualistic competitive society. A free health service is pure Socialism and as such it is opposed to the hedonism of capitalist society." Now look what has happened, the capitalists see the people as a resource to be bled dry and they are doing just that through food pollution and drug anarchy.

CAROLINE: I understand all that, of course, I do think the NHS was a noble and good thing, but things have changed now. Anyway there is no need to be so rude Charles.

SUSAN: It is true Caroline, Matt is an ignorant sod.

CAROLINE: Don't you start you silly young woman.

SUSAN: Listen here you stupid arrogant bitch. Just don't you try to throw your weight around ok.

CAROLINE: Well really! I have never been so insulted!

MATT: Now see what you have done. Filling everyone's head with all that rubbish, You ought to be ashamed of yourself. Someone ought to take that iaptop off you.

SUSAN: Just let them try. Why would you two want to do that I wonder?

ACT TWO, SCENE THREE -

New meeting room the ex-theatre space in the community centre.

JAMES: (*re-enters almost immediately*) Right you lot, I don't know what has been going on here, but it is about time you all heard some home truths and you knuckled down and listened to me. SHUT UP Charlie. Right are you ready Caroline. CAROLINE! ARE YOU ready? As chair I am going to take us through the agenda, with no interruptions. Understood? We will then go through each agenda item in orderly fashion and by the end of the meeting we will have made decisions for this charity. I have been appalled by your behaviour both just now and during the last meeting and I do not expect a repeat of it from now on. (pause) You know listening to you put me in mind of Harold Pinter's famous Nobel Prize winners speech back in 2005.

He said *'the majority of politicians, on the evidence available to us, are interested not in truth but in power and in the maintenance of that power. To maintain that power it is essential that people remain in ignorance, that they live in ignorance of the truth, even the truth of their own lives. What surrounds us therefore is a vast tapestry of lies, upon which we feed'*

I believe that despite the enormous odds which exist, unflinching, unswerving, fierce intellectual determination, as citizens, to define the real truth of our lives and our societies is a crucial obligation which devolves upon us all. It is in fact mandatory.

If such a determination is not embodied in our political vision we have no hope of restoring what is so nearly lost to us - the dignity of man".

You've all got to wake up and focus on the reason we are all here, to manage a charity not run a debating club or a lecture hall. Talk has to be matched by action at least some of the bloody time.

CHARLIE: I mentioned that earlier James.

JAMES: I am very interested in the arts and theatre actually. It is an important part of my life and I find great solace in them especially serious drama. Well just because I'm ex-army doesn't mean I have no brain or intellect.

CHARLIE: You have to have brains to be in the army. My grandad was in World War One. He was a clever one.

MATT: Harold who? Never heard of him.

CAROLINE: He was a coward.

JAMES: What?

CAROLINE: I heard somewhere at a party say they thought he refused to do his National Service. Never trust a man who won't fight.

JAMES: He did write damn good plays.

CHARLIE: Actually he wasn't anti-war just anti-the Cold War, which was no war at all.

MATT: What is the Cold War? I never heard of that one in school. It must have been unimportant.

CHARLIE: What do the young learn at school? How to write rap music I suppose. At least there is a steady supply of reality TV fodder from that curriculum subject. The Cold War, for all your information, was a continuing state of military and political tension between the Western World and The Soviet states.

The word comes from the stand off occasioned by both parties having nuclear weapons, i.e. A cold war, not a hot active war.

MATT: Why did they bother? Why not just sue for peace? Sounds like a lot posturing to me.

SUSAN: I guess you'd know about that Matt. Everyone knows what the Cold War was surely?

CHARLIE: What's your favourite Pinter piece, James?

JAMES: 'The Room' . No, I mean' No Man's Land, of course.

CHARLIE: Really mine is The Go-Between. I remember Julie Christie was in the film version. An acquaintance of my cousin's worked on the costumes for that play. It was set in Edwardian times and bit in the 1970's with an old man reminiscing about his youth and how good it was looking back.

JAMES: It wasn't all good though was it.

CAROLINE: I thought we were getting down to business.

JAMES: Yes sorry Charlie, let's talk later if you like. (*collecting his papers together*) So. The agenda.

Number 1 - Those present and apologies
Number 2 - Minutes of the meeting before last
Number 3 - The Financial report
Number 4 - The Future
Number 5 - AOB

I just need to say now that you must all think bloody long and hard about the new funding.

SUSAN: Is it all settled then?

JAMES: Well no of course not but Fuzzy Products are great and I am personally pleased with their service so far. Even my 'treatment resistance' pills are working. I am doing well. It could be a good thing for us to have a strong pharmaceutical company taking an interest in us and our service users.

SUSAN: But there are lot of serious things to consider before we do that.

CAROLINE: Oh shut up Susan, give James a chance to speak.

JAMES: Charlie, you have a good point when you say there could be a conflict of interest in putting all our eggs in the Fuzzy basket. I just don't know yet what to think. We all must listen to each other if we are to make a good decision. It may be good to try to imagine what could go wrong with this funder and what could go right.

SUSAN: Well James I think that we do need to think long and hard as getting into bed with Fuzzy, a massive drugs company could be just too 'heavy' for us. It would make for heavy drugs based services I bet and I for one am not in favour.

JAMES: OK I hear you Susan. Well let's just start with those present and have you recorded that Caroline?

CAROLINE: Yes of course!

ENID: She hasn't. She only just wrote it down now, I saw her.

CAROLINE: Telling tales isn't very professional now is it Enid.

JAMES: Ok, minutes of meeting before last, any matters arising?

CHARLIE: I just want to query the budget figures carried forward from my last financial report

MATT: Look Charlie, I had to re-organise the system so as to balance the books and re-allocate funding. We have to sort this problem and I had to manipulate the figures to make us an exciting prospect for funders.

CHARLIE: So cooking the books in fact.

MATT: No, It's just that the accounting system was just a little too transparent.

CHARLIE: And, that's a problem?

MATT: If you want the charity to keep running some of its services, yes.

CHARLIE: I see. Mister Chair, I would like it noted that my closing accounts of March are ratified as a complete and proper account of the charity's financial situation presented to the committee upon my resignation as treasurer.

JAMES: OK (pause) I would like to accept Charlie's final accounts as a true and up to date record of the charity's current financial status. Do I have a seconder?

SUSAN: I second that.

CHARLIE: Thank you all.

ENID: Is it time for food yet? (*crosses to the refreshments table)*

JAMES AND MATT: I don't think so....

MATT: I was about to talk about the finances and the new funders.

CHARLIE: They are not funders yet surely.....

CAROLINE: I really must go and powder my nose (*she passes a look at Matt and exits*)

MATT: Me too..... No, I mean I need the loo. (*exits with Caroline)*

ACT TWO, SCENE FOUR -

New meeting room the ex-theatre space in the community centre.

(*Everyone is back in the room now, the table is laden with evil, poisonous foodstuffs, people are sorting themselves out.)*

MATT: Did anyone get to see any of the Olympics?

SUSAN: Don't talk to me about that waste of money?

CAROLINE: I actually was at the opening ceremony? It was superb, I felt proud to be British.

JAMES: Was it very expensive, your Ladyship? I heard it was a load of bloody "Cor blimey, Mary Poppins, and Double Decker buses, wasn't it?

CAROLINE: Well yes it was rather, but that's not all. It was worth every penny. We really know how to put on a show. There we some very interesting aspects, like the Industrial revolution for one.

CHARLIE: It wasn't as good as the Chinese one though.

CAROLINE: But they had thousands of unpaid people forced to perform in the opening ceremony. It is easy to make a splash when you are a dictatorship, or should I say Communist regime. Thats how the Russians kept the Cold War going so long, because they had so many people under the thumb.

SUSAN: Not much difference there. In fact we seem to be living in one ourselves at the moment

CAROLINE: Susan, what a bizarre thing to say. We have a very fair government at the moment doing what it needs to do to get us out of trouble. We all must pull together in our new

Big Society. David, is doing a great job I think, if only Clegg would let him get on with it. I suppose the socialists need to feel like they have sort of voice.

SUSAN: When you say 'us' , who do you mean? Not me and Enid I think, maybe not many of us here right now, I dare say you'll be ok though. Cos money attracts money and the Olympics attracts money too for those in the know or who can pull some strings. The scandal about the use of the stadium after the Games is typical of this country's apathy towards corruption, it squeals about it for five minutes before something else becomes more newsworthy, the damn rich think they are above the law and can get away with dodgy deals.

CAROLINE: That is terrificly unfair Susan. I know the person you are talking about and she is a very respectable business woman. It's the media who have it in for her. She is so sweet actually and adorable and often organises tickets for the football for my nephews. My husband had some business dealings with her and always said how good she was at her job. It is scandalous how the media go poking about in people's business affairs and start slinging mud before they get the whole story.

SUSAN: No what is scandalous is the fact that even in government there is corruption and double dealing

CAROLINE: Those MP's were within their rights to claim for allowances, they get paid so little for governing this great country,

SUSAN: The House of Commons and even the Lords is often empty when debates are taking place, seems that the lure of Big Brother and Hello magazine is all too much. Big Society is just dressing up massive wholesale cuts with a shift to community governance.

CAROLINE: Where do you get all these terms from Susan? The Open University does fill your head with such claptrap honestly. The Big Society shifts power to the people of course, a step too far in some cases in my view though. (glancing at Enid)

JAMES: So you mean, we'll give the public more power to decide things, make them happy, but provide much less money to put anything into practice, make them responsible for doing nothing in effect. Cloud Bloody cuckoo land as usual. It won't ever affect Cameron either. He'll be on the bloody lecture circuit when he goes even if he is forced out. Look at Thatcher she used to get a million a throw just for spouting her bullshit policies. And bloody Tony Blair. He's paid in the region of £3 million a year to advise both JP Morgan, the US investment bank, and also Zurich International, the global insurer based in Switzerland. On top of that he runs his own consultancy firm - Tony Blair Associates - which advises the oil and gas rich governments of Kuwait and Kazakhstan. Done alright for himself I must say and all that for a Labour Prime Minister.

SUSAN: So called!

CAROLINE: Mr. Cameron is our saviour, he'll be remembered for it. The man who brought the Big Society.

JAMES: Let's hope its a good memory for the posh bugger.

SUSAN: Everyone has two choices: 'sink' or 'swim', oh apart from the poor, the old frail, the I sick and the dependent and of course those on the margins of society like Enid and me.

CHARLIE: I'll be ok. I think I have a good pension. Although nothing is certain these days and ageism is alive and well.

MATT: I could say the same, in reverse of course.

CHARLIE: It's the money men that ruin everything I wish more people would see that. They get everywhere nowadays. It didn't use to be like it. There was a time when sportsmen took part for the joy of it and to honour their country, (taking out his notebook and looking for a reference as he speaks) whereas now they just earn a small fortune and moan about it. That Wayne Rooney earns 16 million a year and in 2010 he didn't kick a football because of injury until the third week in November, yet he still earned £800,000. Do you know it would take most other people, earning £40k a year, 20 years to earn that much. Did you also know that the average annual income in the UK is £26k. And, this man has the gall to ask for our sympathy when his team loses. There is too much emphasis on money per se and too little on giving value for money. He's got a bloody cheek I must say.

MATT: Here we go again. What has Wayne Rooney got to do with our charity? I don't know where you get your figures from anyway. Seems you must spend all your life on the internet uncovering all this conspiracy stuff. What bearing has it on our decision to accept Fuzzy's funding?

CHARLIE: I am interested Matt, in world affairs, not just my own.

ENID: Fancy admitting to having affairs. The man has no shame. Oo-la-la!

CHARLIE: Look where a reliance on credit has taken us all, we are in a global financial meltdown and all the government's can think of is a) more of the same, b) print more money and c) rip off the public to boost the coffers again. We are all supposed to go back to wartime austerity, stiff upper lip and all that. I never thought we would see those days again.

MATT: It's not that bad Charlie.

CHARLIE: How can young people know?

MATT: I think it would be great if 'we' could print more money cos God knows we need a shed load right now to get out of this shit we're in.

CHARLIE: It is really naive to think that we can get out of trouble just by shifting budgets around and letting a multi-national company into this charity, especially one which has been caught operating outside the law. It's stupid to think that either of these things are a long term solution to supporting our service users. This whitewash does not even make sense.

MATT: I've told you all that this is a great solution to our problem.

CHARLIE: It needs to be proved. We need to be convinced, we need the detail. I cannot see it myself.

SUSAN: I agree, I am lost with the new system, it's too vague, let's see the small print and if we as committee members don't get it how can we make a proper decision based on one man's say so.

ENID: I am confused too, but I do want my service to carry on

JAMES: They have a point Matt .

CAROLINE: I think it's despicable of you all to victimise Matt like this. I really do.

MATT: Well if you cannot appreciate my work and don't trust my judgement (*beginning to hyper-ventilate, reaches for his Ventolin)* I really don't know what to say.

(Exit, followed by Caroline)

SUSAN: Oh please, all we were asking for was more detail and a deeper understanding to help us make an informed decision. I think you are right Charlie; it feels like bullshit to me.

ACT TWO, SCENE FIVE -

New meeting room the ex-theatre space in the community centre

ENID: More coffee James? Can I tempt you to a Turkish Delight Mint Cream? No one seems to be eating much today, I really tried hard to get some new things, I even tried a different shop.....

CHARLIE: It looks as though the food is of a similar standard.

JAMES: UGH! Here we go again I suppose.

CHARLIE: My old Gran used to say 'we don't need none of that new fangled packet rubbish' and I agree with her although the world is so over-populated it does seem like we have to make some compromises. Of course the way folks live their lives now also means people haven't got the time to be making food from scratch. The world has gone mad, my Mum never went out to work, she stayed at home and kept house. My wife, or rather my ex-wife did the same. This is in part why society has degenerated into a selfish culture, no stability for kids today; they know they come third or fourth in the hierarchy of demand on their parents. Somewhere after work, social life and shopping I think and even after the telly in a lot of cases. There's just no respect anymore, if a teacher can't smack a kid or even restrain it in an emergency situation, how can we expect kids to know any boundaries. Argh, and that's another thing, what is the use of spending hours negotiating with your kid to get them to put a coat on when we should have been somewhere three hours ago. Just how many times is a person going to ask nicely before they blow up or have a breakdown. Parents used to have powers now all they have is wasted breath and burn out. The thing is if you look at it all, it's the capitalists who are actually to blame, they want to sell their products so they change the society's views on parenting and on the makeup of the family. This leads to every room in a house having a TV and a computer and one of those new fangled Kindle things. For God's sake read a book, have dinner together and talk, but no. Most people follow the me - me culture and live their own lives, leaving their kids to their own entertainment, which makes them unruly anyway. All those clever adverts with little kids telling their parents off and violence peddled in all kids media. If you are thinking of yourself the last thing you need is someone telling you you should spend time on educating your kids when they are at home. Heaven forbid! And another thing....

CAROLINE: (*Enters*) When you have quite finished, Charlie, I think you ought to come and say sorry to Matt. He won't come back in until you do.

SUSAN: Oh yippee.

CAROLINE: You think it's funny Susan?

SUSAN: No! I was talking about the scones. They look delicious Enid!

CAROLINE: Oh I see well Charlie what about it? Are you man enough to say sorry?

CHARLIE: Of course I will. Maybe I was a little over the top.

JAMES: (*agitated*) Bloody hell! Can we try to move on soon? Do what you have to do Charlie and let's get on.

SUSAN: Matt is such a cry baby, honestly. If he were professional and remotely knew what he was doing he would be able to face out Charlie's and my criticism.

ENID: My dad used to call my mum a cry-baby, when she'd had one gin too many. She used to get maudlin with it. She'd cry a lot and lock herself away upstairs. I always preferred tea, but I know other people love a drink, that's ok for them. Cup of tea anyone? A cup of tea always makes the world seem like a better place.

JAMES: Or at least a good excuse to have a biscuit or a cake. Just while we're waiting, of course.

ENID: Well there is that I suppose.

SUSAN: Seems like you are busted Enid. HA!

JAMES: Where did they get to? Can you go and find out how they are doing? I really don't need this now.

SUSAN: Of course, I'll be back in a mo (*exits*)

ACT TWO, SCENE SIX -

New meeting room the ex-theatre space in the community centre.

ENID: (*to Susan*) You know it seems to me, that everywhere I've been imprisoned, I mean given asylum, that those in charge seem to have less sense and more troubles than the so-called patients.

JAMES: Ha! I think you have a point there.

SUSAN: It does seem to be that way. I look at how so called sane people operate and I wonder. I suppose all the madness started in the Victorian times with all those terrible places they put up to house the lunatics and idiots, I learnt about all this last year in my course. My God they were hideous places. I was reading about some of the massive asylums that were built, some with 3 miles of corridors, their own farms and churches even, but the conditions for patients were dreadful, and some of the treatments barbaric.

JAMES: There had to be somewhere to house all these people though. You couldn't have thousands of mental patients roaming the streets and they needed help which it was best to give in the confines of a hospital.

SUSAN: Some of the help included bloodletting, purging, hot and cold baths and even a tranquiliser chair was developed at one time, used to tie a person up and covering their eyes and head with a box. More suitable in a horror film these days. Very nice!

JAMES: That was years ago Susan, it doesn't apply any more.

ENID: Out of sight, out of mind. That's what my Mum and Dad wanted, I know that now.

SUSAN: Those two things go together even now, don't you find? We are not supposed to talk about our illness, not really. That's the price for not being out of sight anymore. But, of course, we do talk about it more and more. We are all being encouraged to 'Come Out' about mental illness, about time too.

ENID: It is great to have someone to talk to. It was all I really wanted during all those years of medication and E.C.T. We were nothing better than dogs it seemed. You know we used to be lined up absolutely naked and hosed down instead of allowed baths, it was awful, at least it was women only, just once every two weeks.

SUSAN: I never had to face that thank God. You and me both regards the talking though, we just needed someone to help us work it all out eh? A good old gossip does the trick eh?

ENID: Especially over a cup of tea and a slice of Battenburg, HA!

JAMES: Yes, but what's to bloody talk about, there are drugs now, drugs make the dreadful things go away. My drugs really help get me through the bad times.

SUSAN: They don't send the pain away though, they just dampen it, make it bearable. We just don't know what all the drugs do to us either. So rarely does society look at itself and say 'hey, have we got any part in this rise in mental ill health'. It's interesting don't you think that the upsurge in the need for massive asylums coincides neatly with the dawn of the Industrial Revolution?

JAMES: All this is academic crap though, ivory tower stuff spouted by those mop headed bloody intellectuals. What matters to people is 'happiness'. No one wants to be sad.

SUSAN: There is a difference I think between having mental ill health and feeling a bit low today. Wouldn't you say Enid?

JAMES: But my medication helps me cope with life. I do get down, you know and panicky .

SUSAN: But you haven't seen anyone to look at why? Not even a doctor?

JAMES: Bloody doctors! I don't need them poking their nose in my business. Bloody fools the lot of them, they don't know what they are talking about, at least the Pharma companies tell you symptoms and give you a choice. I saw what my trouble was straight away. I didn't need to bloody talk to anyone, now I just get on with life.

SUSAN: It looks to me like you could use some help (gently smiling) why do you think the Pharma companies help you to think about your symptoms? Because they miraculously have the solution in their medications. These online companies have only been around for 20 years or so but self diagnosis is all the rage these days. We are all supposed to have an inviolable choice to decide for ourselves about our health, but only if you use the Big Pharmas products.

ENID: That's like my old mum and the eggs from Mr Gunhouse. (*pause*) You do look poorly James. Do you want another piece of cake or a sausage roll?

SUSAN: I am not sure that that would be better than taking another tablet really. You heard what's in all that processed sweet stuff.

ENID: He needs to get his blood sugar up. I read that somewhere, when someone is feeling faint or panicky, it's a good boost.

SUSAN: Sugar is bad Enid, it really is!

ENID: Oh, sweet, that'll make you feel better (*James takes a large slice of Battenburg*) See, he knows what is good for him, don't you James.

JAMES: Well it can't do any harm I suppose. My Mum used to give me Battenburg whenever my Dad was on the rampage, oh and Wagon Wheels too and even delicious chip butties. I never stooped so low as to eating deep fried mars bars or pizzas though.

ENID: Oh I love all that exotic food, it is definitely better than the cabbage soup I used to have in Ashill, You know even the walls in the corridors and the heavy plastic concertina doors were Cabbage Green. And the smell of the place, well you can just imagine what the atmosphere was like.

ACT TWO, SCENE SEVEN -

New meeting room the ex-theatre space in the community centre.

(Charlie, Matt and Caroline enter)

JAMES: Welcome back you three. Have you sorted your differences out? Are we ready to discuss the future?

MATT: I am ready, most definitely.

CHARLIE: Go ahead.

MATT: As I was saying earlier we were approached by Fuzzy Pharma Ltd a couple of weeks ago.

CHARLIE: We? Who is we?

JAMES: Charlie give him a chance. Let's save questions for later. Matt go ahead.

MATT: As I was saying.... We were approached by Fuzzy with a suggestion for us to join their help in the community campaign called A Bright Future! This scheme enables mental health charities to survive the funding freeze which so many organisations find themselves having to deal with. It makes a lot of sense.....Fuzzy is amongst the top pharmaceutical companies in the world and they pride themselves on their ability to provide focussed health care for their millions of clients. They recognise that good health is vital to all of us, they are really committed to this. They are a leading research pharmaceutical company which has to count for something.

SUSAN: So we can be their guinea pigs is that it? They'd have a ready market here. I remember now they haven't got a very good reputation in the HIV field especially in Africa. There combination retroviral medications got through the FDA at break neck speed but at a price that no one in the developing world can afford. An English friend of mine is on them and he says that they cost £1000 a month.

CAROLINE: Thats disgusting.

SUSAN: Yes, it puts the developing world at such a disadvantage.

CAROLINE: No I mean that someone with a disease they could have avoided should bleed the NHS of so much money.

SUSAN: Oh please, you stupid woman, get yourself out of the dark ages.

ENID: I had a guinea pig at Ashill, Jemmy was its name. I named it after a Russian Princess' dog. They dug its body up when the Royal Family were murdered.

CHARLIE: But were they....two bodies were missing when they found that group in a grave outside Ekaterinburg. They had all sorts of DNA tests done, I think they used Prince Philip's DNA.

ENID: It must be right if his DNA says so.

CHARLIE: But the numbers still didn't add up. One of the daughters and the young Tsarevich's bodies are missing still. So the Russian and European Royal tack saying that all the family died, has definite flaws in it. I always believed that Anna Anderson woman, you know the one who said she was Grand Duchess Anastasia.

ENID: The dog definitely died though, they proved it.

SUSAN: Enid please..... This is serious.

ENID: I'm sorry, I thought we were talking about animals.

MATT: Look Susan, everyone. It's not like that at all. They are committed to their patients, customers and shareholders.

CHARLIE: Argh! The shareholders. We all know what shareholders mean, I assume. Anyway, for those who are unaware, shareholders mean a financial trap with companies making decisions based on the needs of their shareholders first and foremost. What do shareholders want? They want a return on their investment of course.

MATT: They are committed to ensure transparency in their dealings and have the highest ethical standards.

CHARLIE: So what does all that company speak mean?

SUSAN: What does it mean for me and Enid? We need to know what that all means for the service users and for the organisation. What strings are attached? What are they asking for in order to save our organisation?

ENID: Yeah I want to know I am safe but also what we all have to do to be safe?

CHARLIE: I hope there are some answers to these questions.

CAROLINE: It seems like you are all against Matt. It is so awful of you to treat him like this. He is doing his best. We may not have him for much longer, I imagine he will get a job very soon.

MATT: I am committed to the charity, I'll be sticking around.

CHARLIE: We are being sold Fuzzy.

MATT: When Fuzzy give us the money it will all become clear. We need this funding and we need it now. We cannot go on much longer without it.

SUSAN: Is there anything else we need to know Matt?

MATT: What do you mean?

SUSAN: Well I cannot believe that Fuzzy won't expect other things. My OU course materials are littered with examples of this sort of thing where charities sell themselves down the river, unknowingly of course or rather stupidly.

MATT: Well they do require a new management structure, they expect a new director to liaise with their marketing and sales team, and need some board members co-opted from their board. There is nothing to be afraid of Susan.

SUSAN: You keep saying that Matt. But I am not convinced. It sounds fishy to me. I am definitely against it.

CHARLIE: It is hard to comprehend.

CAROLINE: I cannot believe you people. You have a solution before you, why not take it?

JAMES: I'm sure that's not what he meant at all. I suggest that to get beyond this impasse we have a vote, before we run out of time today.

ENID: Well, it is worrying. It really is. I don't know what to think.

CAROLINE: Enid dear maybe Charlie is right you might need to be excused from the decision, if you are unsure and if you do as Charlie said, have a 'conflict of interest'.

JAMES: That is not something you can decide Caroline.

ENID: What do you mean Caroline?

CAROLINE: Maybe you shouldn't vote Enid. We don't want to worry you.

CHARLIE: We cannot disbar anyone from being part of the decision making process, not without good reason and having a learning disability or mental ill health is not one of them. Our service user reps would be disbarred, which would make a mockery of service user involvement. What I actually said had people been listening....

CAROLINE: I am ever so slightly sick of listening Charlie.

CHARLIE: Let me finish please.....As I was saying, all that we all, service users reps included, have to make sure of, is that we make a decision based on full facts and details presented to us.

ENID: I don't understand it all Matt

MATT: All you need to know Enid, because of your disability, is that your service will be safe with Fuzzy and without them the future of the organisation and your services is in grave doubt. So best thing to do is to defer to the professionals those who have done their homework.

SUSAN: You don't have to take that shit from these two Enid. Don't be bullied.

CAROLINE: Susan that's not very useful to take away Enid's hope of a safe future. What is your alternative?

SUSAN: My alternatives is to search for alternatives, has anyone considered that the organisation is not viable and maybe should close down and allow other impartial organisations to take on the service load.

MATT: That's pissy liberal hogwash. It's mad! You'd have to be mental to think that is the best way forward.

SUSAN: So I'd have to be mental is that what you are saying?

JAMES: Come on everyone let's vote. Those in favour of Fuzzy funding us?

MATT: Me for sure.

CAROLINE: Me too.

ENID: Erm, yes!

SUSAN AND CHARLIE: No. No.

JAMES: So its down to me. Bloody hell!! We have thanks to Charlie and Susan, an idea about just some of the things are happening in the world, the way that we are all being manipulated by the damn multi-national companies under the guise of making our lives easier. It is true that we may have a conflict of interest if we accept Fuzzy's offer of funding, and that could be difficult for us in the future, it even could mean the closure of the charity in the future if we feel we cannot continue to get support from a company who sells a product that our service users need. This seems to be a major stumbling block to us accepting the funds from Fuzzy. but I am afraid though that I must vote in favour of Fuzzy, (he reaches into his pocket for a pill, a Fuzzy Pharma pill) we clearly have no choice in the matter, we are beaten and this is a golden opportunity to get back on track.

SUSAN: See, they kick us when we are down and get inside a charity to boost their sales.

MATT: WOW hurrah we are saved ! Just you wait and see everything will be great.

CAROLINE: Super Matt!

ENID: Shall I make another drink.......(*Susan takes out her laptop.)*

JAMES: Yes let's bloody celebrate: the saving of the charity!. Right, I have to go to the loo again. (*exits.)*

(Charles follows Enid to the refreshments, Matt and Caroline stay at the table,Susan goes off alone.)

ACT TWO, SCENE EIGHT -

New meeting room the ex-theatre space in the community centre.

JAMES: RIGHT. I suggest that Matt and I should liaise with Fuzzy to sort out the finer points and that we should then report back to you all in September.

MATT: Sounds good to me.

JAMES: Cheer up Susan, this is great news for us all.

SUSAN: Is it? *(Susan gets up and taking her laptop goes to a corner of the room*)

ENID: I got some Sunny Delight, I thought we could mix it with lemonade for a Bucks Fizz. Go all swanky like my old mum used to. Dad didn't like mum having a tipple.

CAROLINE: Oh please Enid, That stuff is really such shit darling.

CHARLIE: It is shit, but people are trying their best, a little of what you fancy as I said before

CAROLINE: Don't be a sore loser, Charles.

CHARLIE: We were all supposed to be winners.

CAROLINE: You know what I mean. If James had voted the other way we still would have had deadlock

MATT: Drop it please.

JAMES: Come and join us Susan, for a toast

SUSAN: HA!HA!HA! You but you might want to hold off the toast for a moment or two.

JAMES: What do you mean? (*everyone looks towards Susan*)

SUSAN: (*crosses back to table*). Please come back everyone. I have a question for someone in the group. Matt would you like tell people about your new job?'

MATT: Oh. Well. Well! James is the meeting over now? I have to be on my way I think. (*Matt exits quickly*)

(*Susan holds up her laptop, with a picture of Matt on the screen, but puts it down as she watches Matt run away, everyone's attention is on Matt as he leaves urgently*)

ENID: SUNNY DELIGHT ANYONE?

BLACKOUT

ACT THREE, SCENE ONE -

Same old meeting room, two months later, the ex-theatre space in the community centre has been cleared out it is an empty room.

CAROLINE: Well, this is an improvement! Pretty empty though but the cleaner was obviously using a dirty cloth, (*running her fingers over surfaces*) I am not surprised really, the people from the estate would not know any better. What has happened to the Big Society we planned for everyone? Oh yes! You have to have honest, hardworking and submissive citizens for that. What am I saying citizens?

ARCHIE: I agree Caroline there is no way to educate plebs into model citizens who give a damn about anyone else. It wasn't like that in our day.

CAROLINE: I am surprised a young man like you can remember those times.

ARCHIE: We're not all stupid ignoramuses you know? I was brought up properly, knowing my social responsibility and what is right from wrong. You would never find me swindling anyone out of their money or property, climbing on their back to get an advantage or hurting another person just for a laugh,

CAROLINE: Nor me. That sort of behaviour is reprehensible. You know it was such good fortune to meet you at that MIND art exhibition. I call it fortuitous and to meet a fellow art enthusiast is so exciting. I do hope you do not get put off by the others on the Management Committee.

ARCHIE: I can hold my own believe me. I am a great believer in synchronicity and I do so want to put something back into the community to stem the flow of all this wickedness.

CAROLINE: Yes you are right it is a huge task to clear up the streets and the estates, around here and around the country generally. Everything has gotten out of hand. There is thievery everywhere you look. One is quite scared truthfully.

ARCHIE: Yes it is insidious to see how easily the nation has slumped to an all time low. I don't know what our PM can do about it? He will have to commit to ensuring the whole country knows what will happen if things don't change.

CAROLINE: Well he is being strong and the people, I mean the masses, have got the idea now that things have to get worse before they get better. We all have to pull together. (*pause*) Do watch out for Enid, she will smother you with the most awful food and with her reminiscences of life in the old asylums, but she means well. I believe as we now have a bigger budget we may even have been able to persuade her to go up a notch in the gourmet stakes!

ARCHIE: Are the meetings run quite well? Or as I am guessing is at all a bit hit and miss?

CAROLINE: The latter. My, you are clever and insightful.

ARCHIE: Well it will be interesting, I cannot bear that kind of time wasting. What is the chair like? Does he have issues around asserting himself?

CAROLINE: He can get a bit uptight but he does have a lot to contend with. He did though successfully guide us through the decision to accept Fuzzy Pharma funding, eventually that is. He has been working furiously since then with Matt, who was our treasurer but is now the liaison development worker for Fuzzy. He will be here later to present the final proposal and supervise us all in signing it.

ARCHIE: So I am replacing this man Matt?

CAROLINE: He is such a nice young man and has done a lot for the charity. In fact he has been instrumental in saving us.

ARCHIE: He sounds like a proper young man, one you would trust with anything.

CAROLINE: Oh yes, he is a trustworthy sort and a strong realist, not one of those terrible PC people who muddle up charity with rights. That road leads to anarchy, do you not agree?

ARCHIE: Oh yes! And we cannot have anarchy. Look what resulted in those riots a while back.

CAROLINE: Indeed, I rest my case.

ACT THREE, SCENE TWO –

Same old meeting room, two months later, the ex-theatre space in the community centre has been cleared out it is an empty room.

JAMES: Oh, hello Caroline, so this must be Archie, pleased to meet you. I am James the Chair. Shall we have a quick chat before the meeting starts? Let's go over there.

ENID: Oh hello Caroline, hello James, Oh hello. I am Enid. Nice to meet you, you must be Albert, isn't it?

ARCHIE: Archie actually. Nice to meet you too, I've heard a lot about you.

JAMES: Enid, please I need to have a quick......

ENID: Caroline, guess what? We got some extra money from Fuzzy so I went to S & M, what do you say to that? Better than Iceland isn't it? You used to tell me off for going to that place. What was it you used to call them?.

CAROLINE: That doesn't matter dear. They are better than Iceland to some degree, but really you can only be sure of the best if things are not processed and as fresh as possible

ENID: What like your mushrooms you mean? How is your tapeworm these days?. HE! HE! HE!

CAROLINE: Oh very funny. They are OK I suppose, they are still known for their e-numbers though and as for the pig fat in their trifle, horrid!

ENID: What? This has pig fat in it? But it's a pudding, you wouldn't put pig fat in a sweet surely?

CAROLINE: Well they do. Give me that trifle

ENID: It's for later

CAROLINE: No give it here, let me see the list of ingredients.So here we are; listen to this..........

JAMES: Shall we?

ARCHIE: Just a minute, this is interesting.

JAMES: I would like to have a chat before the trouble makers get here.

CAROLINE: There are certainly some dodgy things in this. Maltodextrin, emulsifiers, gelling agents, red colouring, E415, sodium citrate, E414, trisodium citrate, tetrasodium diphosphate, dicalcium phosphate, E407 and E471 potassium sorbate. Oh, and here its is pork fat, bold as anything. A serving gives you nearly 24g of your daily 90g of sugar as sugar, dextrose and strawberry juice concentrate, plus 9g saturated fat. It is terrible stuff.

ARCHIE: I must say I make my own usually.

ENID: It's not so bad as that milk shake. I couldn't even count the number of things in that.

JAMES: Archie, lets go *next door* for a chat.

ARCHIE: NO! Here is ok

JAMES: Let's go over there then. Just out of the way of Enid particularly. She has limited understanding, bless her.Caroline, could you take Enid down to the post office before we start, we need some more flipchart pens?

CAROLINE: Oh alright, do we need anything else?

ENID: I am busy James, there is a lot to do to prepare for the party later. I am looking forward to seeing Matt. I like working with him. He is lovely. He is a star for getting us out of the shit, as my old Dad would say.

JAMES: Enid, it was he who asked for new flipchart pens, all colours too. He needs them for his presentation later. Use what is left of the petty cash. Caroline will go to help you.

ENID: Oh OK, If you put it like that, I suppose it is more important right now.

CAROLINE: Come on Enid, let us go. The men need to sort out some business together!

ENID: We can sort stuff out too. We *women* I mean. Come on. (*they exit.)*

ACT THREE - SCENE THREE –

Same old meeting room, two months later, the ex-theatre space in the community centre has been cleared out it is an empty room.

JAMES: It is great to have you on board Archie.

ARCHIE: Thanks James.

JAMES: I don't know how much Caroline has told you? She said you were on side though with the decision we have come to, the one to accept Fuzzy Pharma's support.

ARCHIE: Yes it does seem like a very good idea. We all have to bend to the wind in these difficult times. It is the bottom line.

JAMES: And, we can all benefit too, I mean each of us can, if you know what I mean?

ARCHIE: Well why don't you tell me a little about that? I am always interested in some benefits when volunteering. It can't do any harm.

JAMES: Well, take Enid for instanc. She is much happier as we have a bigger budget for entertaining and she loves that and is now able to get better food, and she gets to take home what we don't eat which means a lot to her. She is very happy with Fuzzy.

ARCHIE: I can imagine. At grassroots level Fuzzy's offer is going make a lot of difference to people who use the services. So what else? Who else benefits?

JAMES: Well Caroline is going to undertake some training paid for by Fuzzy and will do some national research for us.

She'll get to visit other charities who may be helped out by Fuzzy in the future - a sort of ambassador. She has really started to develop her skills since Fuzzy took over.

ARCHIE: Oh, have they taken over already? I didn't realise.

JAMES: Well no, but bar the shouting, it is a done deal. The funding that is. Of course, we'll still be managing the project and its services. We'll sign this afternoon during the second part of the meeting. Fuzzy have been setting things in place for us for the last two months that's all. You'll meet Matt later.

ARCHIE: What about the other MC members, Susan and Charlie is it? What do they get out of the new funding?

JAMES: Well, lots if they'd only stop putting up barriers to the new scheme. Ever since it was first mooted they have been against it. I don't know what they think is the alternative. They both bang on about conflicts of interest.

ARCHIE: Surely a Pharma company is a good thing to have funding a mental health charity. How else do you ensure cheap medication for people? Fuzzy have been in the field for years so they know what they are taking about.

JAMES: That's my point exactly, but they think we will be sold down the river, be overrun with corporate men and be closed down once he dust settles. They are both a bit weird. I just wanted to warn you. Charlie is a busybody and Susan has a massive chip on her shoulder. She is another user rep. like Enid.

ARCHIE: Oh yes I know the type: jobsworths.

JAMES: Too right! Oh and Charlie can bore for Britain, be warned, especially if he thinks you remotely give a damn about what he is talking about. He is then like a dog with a bone.

ARCHIE: My uncle Archie, an unfortunate namesake, is exactly the same. You can't shut him up once he starts HA! HA! HA! (pause) And....what do you get out of all this James?

JAMES: Well between you and me, I do have a bit of an anxiety problem and I was, before all this kicked off, buying Fuzzy anti-depressants and treatment resistant drugs from them online, but now (*pause*) I have a guaranteed supply for life. I don't do counselling, that's what people tried to get me into, I know these pills work and they keep me steady so hey, why not make the most of it?

ARCHIE: Why not indeed!

ACT THREE, SCENE FOUR –

Same old meeting room, two months later, the ex-theatre space in the community centre has been cleared out it is an empty room.

CHARLIE: Hello, James. You haven't been returning my calls......

JAMES: Oh, Charlie, can you give me a minute, please! I am just having a briefing chat with our new recruit.

CHARLIE: Oh, hello, I heard we had a new member. I'm Charlie, I used to be the treasurer on the committee.

JAMES: Yes, Charlie thank you.

ARCHIE: Hello there, I am pleased to meet you. I have heard about you from Caroline.

JAMES: Oh well I think we had better get the others in, thanks for the chat, Archie. Can you get the others Charlie?

CHARLIE: Yes, but we can't start yet.

JAMES: Why not? We have a lot to do today.

CHARLIE: Susan isn't here yet and we can'tstart without her.

JAMES: Oh she can catch up.

CHARLIE: I'll give her a call, she must be on her way.

JAMES: No need to do that surely? She knows what time the meeting is and if she isn't here then its tough. Get a move on please Charlie.

CHARLIE: No! I am going to call Susan I won't be long (*walking out*)

JAMES: Ladies, we are ready to start.

ARCHIE: Maybe we should wait for Susan?

JAMES: Archie, as I said we have a lot to get through. Susan is a bit unreliable at best of times. She is a user rep. you know. Ah! Ladies good to see you, is everything ready?

CAROLINE: I have my tablet at the ready. It was so good of you to organise a Fuzzy tablet for me.

ENID: I haven't had time to sort out the food and drinks yet James. Can I have ten minutes?

JAMES: No, sorry we have a lot of ground to cover today, and we must get the preliminary things done before Matt and Mr Underwood from Fuzzy arrive.

ENID: Well you wont get the refreshments sorted unless I have enough time to lay everything out

JAMES: OK! OK! Just carry on and we'll start and you can listen as you organise things.

CHARLIE: We had best not start in the circumstances. I just spoke to Susan and her notification for the meeting is dated for tomorrow. Seems very odd.

JAMES: She must be confused Charlie, you know what she is like, always getting the wrong end of the stick.

CHARLIE: Not this time James. She took a photo with her phone and I am waiting for her to send it. Iteems she is no way as confused as you would have us all believe.

JAMES: Enid. Carry on sorting the refreshments out love, it's gonna be one of those meetings, I can tell.

ENID: Oh great! I do love sorting stuff out and now that I have S & M stuff its even more exciting.

CHARLIE: So James, why have you not been returning my calls?

JAMES: Oh shut up Charlie! I have more important things to do than to answer every enquiry you have.

CHARLIE: I am sure you have! But my questions are as valid as anyone else's especially if we are to sign away the charity and sell out the users.....

JAMES: Oh stop being so melodramatic. You see far to much into things. I think the internet should be banned to the over 60's

CHARLIE: Oh wait a minute this must be Susan's text with the photo. (pause) Interesting, look everyone Susan's notification is dated tomorrow. I assume as the rest of us are here that somehow Susan's attendance has been blocked. No worries though - Susan was in town today and she will be here in ten minutes.

JAMES: Well we had better wait for her I suppose.......

ENID: Who wants some S & M (*looking at the label*) erm..... sausage roll with their drink.....

ACT THREE, SCENE FIVE –

Same old meeting room, two months later, the ex-theatre space in the community centre has been cleared out it is an empty room.

JAMES: What is she doing? Why isn't she here yet? I thought she was in town already? Bloody hell.

SUSAN: I am here James, I'd like to say I am sorry I am late but, as you are aware, I am in fact, a day early.

JAMES: Yes (*pause*) I am sorry about that, I don't know how that happened?

SUSAN AND CHARLIE: I wonder.

ARCHIE: Hello, I am Archie, the new management committee member.

SUSAN: Happy to....

CAROLINE: He is a friend of mine. We met at a MIND exhibition, didn't we. Archie?

ARCHIE: Yes, we did Caroline.

CAROLINE: I persuaded him that we needed people like him to support us through the new Fuzzy phase.

SUSAN:As I tried to say, I am happy to meet you. That is so nice of you, Caroline, to think of the charity like that.

JAMES: Right enough of these pleasantries, we had better get on.

SUSAN: I have something to say before we start.

JAMES: Not now Susan, you'll get a chance later, please we have to get through things before Matt and Mr Underwood get here.

SUSAN: More like Mr Underhand if you ask me.

JAMES: Don't be disrespectful Susan please.

SUSAN: Well, really why can't you look beyond the end of your nose?

CHARLIE: Leave it Susan! For now let's hear what the man has to say. It seems that he has been very busy since the last meeting, too busy to return my calls and making a silly mistake over the date of the meeting on your letter. Dear me James, you ought to take it easy.

JAMES: Thank you Charlie. Good to see someone has some common sense and common decency.

SUSAN: Phfffff

CHARLIE: So, James, let us hear what you have been up to since the last meeting.

CAROLINE: I don't think that is very nice Charlie. James has been working very hard to pursue the Fuzzy offer. And, I have to say, so have I, in my own way. It takes a lot to sit through and record in writing, important meetings where complicated concepts are being discussed.

CHARLIE: So you can explain to us what is going on with the Fuzzy bid? Let us hear it from you Caroline.

CAROLINE: Well, James or better still, Matt are the best people to talk you through it, which is what James is trying to do right now, if you'd give him a chance.

CHARLIE: Please, please go ahead, O Wise One. I long to know what Fuzzy have in store for us once we have signed on the dotted line.

ENID: You know (*shouting from the table where she has been organising the refreshments*) I think of the company every time I open some of this delicious stuff (opening some lemonade) Fuzzy equals Fizzy. HA! HA!

CAROLINE: Oh please Enid to take this seriously!

ENID: Well, everyone is *so* serious. S & M anyone? It's Battenburg you know. You all liked it at that meeting before, and their cakes are even better than Iceland's.

JAMES: Enid, please shut up, it is not time for refreshments yet.

CHARLIE: Well actually we haven't had a drink yet at all. (To *Enid*) Mine is a cup of Earl Grey, please.

ENID: Oh yippee! Coming up Charlie. Susan what would you like.

SUSAN: Hemlock at this rate!

CAROLINE: What?

SUSAN: Oh nothing Caroline. We cannot expect you to know about poisons can we. You clearly have no idea about some of the more modern ones either.

CAROLINE: I DO know what hemlock is actually, but I don't know why you would choose that one. It is poisonous after all. I am not clear what you are getting at.

ENID: My mum used to love that fizzy drink what was it called again.....Dandelion and Hemlock. Sorry Susan, I didn't think to get that. I never liked it and, as my dear old Dad used to always say, it was an acquired taste anyway.

SUSAN: You can say that again Enid.

ENID: You can get Hemlock down S & M's as well.

ARCHIE: Sounds all too risqué for words if you ask me. HA!

ENID: What would you like Archie?

ARCHIE: Coffee is my poison Enid. Milk and four sugars please.

JAMES: Ok lets have a short break.

ARCHIE: (whispering to James) I see what you mean!

CHARLIE: Fill us in Archie?

SUSAN: Yes do tell us what is so funny?

ARCHIE: Oh nothing I was just giggling at Enid's jokes, forgive me. You're a comedian Enid, really you are, I love it.

ENID: Well, thank you Archie. People often laugh at my jokes. Thing is I never know what's so funny, oh except Fuzzy and Fizzy, I know that's funny.

SUSAN: The things that you say Enid *would* be funny if they weren't so serious.

CAROLINE: Oh do stop picking on Enid, Susan. The poor dear is trying her best to understand, bless her

SUSAN: Patronising cow.

JAMES: Now Susan, no need to start calling each other names. I think you might like to apologise to Caroline.

SUSAN: What for? It's true. That kind of attitude befuddled Enid's view point at the last meeting. Oh yes, that, and some committed bullying if I remember correctly.

CAROLINE: Well, really!

SUSAN: Raw nerve Caroline?

CAROLINE: I do apologise for all this Archie, I hope you won't be put off. Wait a minute that's what we must do first James. Swear in Archie I mean.

JAMES: Yes you are right, I think we ought to vote to bring Archie onto the committee. Do I have a proposer.....?

CHARLIE: Wait a minute. No disrespect Archie, but we don't know anything about you. Would you like to tell us about your background?

JAMES: You don't need to do that Archie. Charlie, Archie comes highly.....

ARCHIE: No worries. I don't mind. I can tell you something about me and my background. I have a brother who is bi-polar, and it has not been an easy ride with him, let me tell you.

CAROLINE: That's terrible Archie, we are all so sorry

ARCHIE: As a result of that, I got involved in MIND doing some fundraising, which was quite successful. It involved thinking outside the box I must say.

SUSAN: Oh here we go.

ARCHIE: It is very difficult to get and keep funding streams now and we often have to make hard choices.

CAROLINE: Yes, like the one we faced four months ago.

ARCHIE: Since then I have helped a lot of other charities avoid the worst case scenario.

CAROLINE: Good for you. That's great news for us I must say.

SUSAN: Yeah right.

CHARLIE: So what is your professional background?

ARCHIE: I was a hedge fund manager to start with then I got a sales job; nothing too onerous. I needed a change in my life and the traveling salesman's life suited me down to the ground.

CHARLIE: What were you selling? Are you a salesman now?

ARCHIE: I worked for GUSK, the big research pharmaceutical company

SUSAN: Surprise! Surprise!

JAMES: Heard enough?

CHARLIE AND SUSAN: Oh yes.

JAMES: So once again - do I have a proposer?

CAROLINE: I would like to propose Archie Whistler.

JAMES: I would like to second that proposal. Those against? (*pause*) Two against. Enid what do you think?

ENID: Is it time for refreshments?

JAMES: No I mean do you think that Archie would be good on the committee?

ENID: Oh yes, as my old mum used to say: 'He'll do very nicely"

SUSAN: Oh Please.

ENID: Shall we have some more S & M stuff? I mean to celebrate.

SUSAN: Excuse me, I need a break, coming Charlie?

JAMES: We haven't finished yet.

SUSAN: Nor have I, but I need a break from this crap..........
(*Susan leaves.*)

ACT THREE, SCENE SIX –

Same old meeting room, two months later, the ex-theatre space in the community centre has been cleared out it is an empty room.

JAMES: Hello, Matt, welcome. Good to see you again.

MATT: Hello everyone.

CHARLIE: grrr grrr *(mumbling)*

MATT: I am really sorry James, everyone, but Mr Underwood can't be here, but he has asked me to deal with the formalities.

JAMES: Oh well, I suppose you are our point of contact with Fuzzy now anyway.

SUSAN: Too afraid to face us I suspect.

MATT: Not at all He is involved with another charity up north and he has to be there today.

SUSAN: They are making a habit of it then.

JAMES: Erm, hardly a nationwide takeover Susan. Just two charities.

SUSAN: That's all we know! We'll see I suppose.

CHARLIE: So what has been going on in last two months that we should know about?

JAMES: Matt, over to you I think

MATT: Well James, you might want to tell everyone what the last two months have been like. I mean what we have been working on.

SUSAN: A lot by the sound of it. Why did you resign Matt? Tell us that.

MATT: Well, it was thought better that I use my talents as a liaison between Fuzzy and the charity. I am up to speed on all the corporate charity innovations.

CHARLIE: What does that mean exactly? Can you explain it to us mere mortals and in Plain English?

CAROLINE: Don't start again Charlie. You had your chance to put your views across at the last meeting, and you too Susan, and still the vote went against you. So don't be sore losers.

CHARLIE: There you go again Caroline. The whole concept of losing. I do not understand what you are talking about. I was not aware that this was a contest. I have only ever wanted what is best for the charity and its users, nothing else.

SUSAN: Are you enjoying your new laptop Caroline? Who paid for that? Oh yes that's a Fuzzy label on the machine. What does that logo stand for, anyway? Looks like a giant cloud to me. Interesting! Who pays for your trips around the country too?

CAROLINE: The logo stands for the ether, the very essence of being. Fuzzy are committed to making things as purely as possible to match our essence.

SUSAN: Oh yes I remember, how does it go now? *'Fuzzy, getting the essence of things'*

CHARLIE: Still looks like a cloud to me HA!

ARCHIE: HA! Oh, sorry Caroline. Forgive me.

CAROLINE: No one seems to be treating this seriously.

JAMES: Matt over to you. Again.

MATT: Oh OK, well James and I have been meeting up regularly to thrash through the funding proposal for Fuzzy. Oh yes, sorry… Caroline too very kindly agreed to be our minute taker. What has come out of all that is that Fuzzy are going to support this charity out of the trouble they are in.

CHARLIE: How are they going to do that?

MATT: Giving funding of course.

SUSAN: What's in it for them?

CAROLINE: You really must try to trust and to be less cynical. You are both as bad as each other. I don't remember you bringing any other ideas forward at the last meeting.

SUSAN: We couldn't get a word in. And, at the end of the meeting I was gagged.

CAROLINE: Don't be ridiculous! You had plenty of chances to speak. Simple fact is the vote went in our favour.

CHARLIE: 'OUR' favour. This is the about charity isn't it? Or am I missing something?

JAMES: Come on people, let's try to get on shall we. We need to listen and then move on to the signing.

MATT: Don't be too hasty James!

SUSAN: Signing?

CHARLIE: What signing?

JAMES: Come on let Matt speak. (*pause*) DAMN! DAMN!

CHARLIE: What are we supposed to be signing. There is nothing mentioned on the letter we got. Look. Neither of ours make any mention of signing.

SUSAN: What the hell is going on?

JAMES: Bloody bugger! Look, I think we need a break, Enid put the kettle on love, andhow about breaking open some of that delicious food?

SUSAN: So, is someone going to explain what is scheduled to happen here today? Seems some people are in the know and some are not. Enid, what do you think is going to happen today?

JAMES: Enid, come on, don't listen to Susan, chop-chop! Hows that food coming along?

ENID: It's alright James I can answer Susan's question.

JAMES: Caroline, can you help Enid out?

CAROLINE: Yes of course. Enid my dear let me help you There are lot of hungry people here and all this talking is making us all thirsty. Come on, lets get on with it. Don't pay any attention to Susan.

ENID: Get out of my way Caroline. I want to answer Susan. I said *get out my way*.

CAROLINE: Enid, please don't you remember what I said to you before the meeting. We agreed you would focus on the refreshments and just listen to the meeting this time.

SUSAN: Am I hearing this right. Seems like all sorts of skullduggery is occurring. So Enid, tell me what you know about the meeting. Let her speak Caroline!

JAMES: Susan, you are out of order. We need to get on with the meeting.

SUSAN: *I* am out of order? What about Caroline trying to physically restrain Enid? Did you ever work in an institution Caroline? It looks like it to me. You'd give Nurse Ratchett a run for her money.

CHARLIE: Are you OK Enid? Why don't you tell us all what you know about today. James, I think you need to back off, don't you?

JAMES: Damn! Do what you like Enid. For fuck's sake. It doesn't matter anyway, *(shaking and reaching for his meds for first time during the meeting*) I am having a break, I need to get out of here for ten minutes. (he leaves and Matt follows)

ENID: Well, what I know is Matt is gonna tell us what Fuzzy can do for us and then we can all sign to accept the deal. I am going to do a different job after that as Fuzzy want me to be a User Rep on their National Forum. It's a very important job. I get to be consulted and everything.

SUSAN: Do you get to vote on stuff?

ENID: Erm....... Caroline what did they say? I don't remember that bit.

CAROLINE: Oh you stupid senile old woman, can't you understand anything? (*Enid runs out crying and Caroline follows her)*

ACT THREE, SCENE SEVEN –

Same old meeting room, two months later, the ex-theatre space in the community centre has been cleared out it is an empty room.

ARCHIE: So, what exactly *is* your opposition to the Fuzzy funding?

SUSAN: Do you really want to know?

ARCHIE: Yes of course I do. I need to know all sides if I am to support what is right for the charity.

SUSAN: What is right for the charity in your view?

ARCHIE: There is always more than one way to skin a cat?

CHARLIE: Interesting choice of proverb there Archie. The language being used here today is very combative and emotive. Susan and I are only seeking answers.

ARCHIE: I was not being combative Charlie, actually you would know if I was, I think. HA!

SUSAN: Well our view is that we think that there is a conflict of interest both in a) Fuzzy funding a mental health charity when they provide medication for mental health issues and b) in our former treasurer Matt being an employee of Fuzzy even when the funding was first mooted. We are not clear what the pay off will be for Fuzzy either. No one seems willing to tell us anything and you can see how we get sidelined and silenced. I know I am not the most diplomatic of people but I want answers and I think as a management committee member I compromise the charity and myself if I don't ask for them.

ARCHIE: But, you have been kept appraised of all the meetings that have been going on?

SUSAN: We were told at the end of last meeting that Matt and James would be taking care of all the liaising with Fuzzy, that is all. No time frame was given. We thought that today's meeting was for further discussion not a *fait accompli* as it now seems to be.

ARCHIE: Interesting. So do you think that those conflicts of interest can be gotten over?

SUSAN: Maybe they could have been, but it is all so underhand, and not entirely subtle either. There is an arrogance in some of our colleagues which beggars belief.

ARCHIE: I see. As I am a new boy I don't know how I can help. I am surprised to find that there is any dissent here

CHARLIE: What do you mean?

ARCHIE: Oh nothing, it's just I would have expected that Fuzzy would have made sure of full support before moving forward. They wouldn't want egg on the their faces would they, because they obviously are committed to good service and supporting communities. I am just surprised that's all. Maybe they don't know all the facts. Do you think Matt and James might be holding things back from them? I am just a novice but it's strange that Mr Underwood is not here for such an important event.

SUSAN: Well I was gagged at the end of the last meeting, and we haven't had the opportunity yet for me to tell Caroline and Enid about Matt's true relationship to Fuzzy.

ARCHIE: Yes they do seem to have it all stitched up. I guess all I can do is ask some questions in all innocence. They cannot refuse to answer me surely. I don't know how it will end up but I am happy to have a go.

SUSAN: That would be great. Obviously anything we say is taken as sour grapes about losing the vote.

CAROLINE: (*entering*) Now Enid, you know I did not mean it. I am sorry. You do understand though don't you. Archie, I am so sorry about all this. Some people just don't know when to let it go or when to accept defeat.

ARCHIE: I know what you mean. I can be like a dog with a bone when something upsets me or when I see injustice or illegality.

CAROLINE: See Susan, so take heed. All this arguing is very upsetting. The decision has been made and it was fairly done, so let it go.

SUSAN: Are you sure it was fairly done? Do you know all the facts of the matter?

CAROLINE: I know that Matt is a good man, and that he has done the right thing in leaving the committee. James is doing the very best to save the charity which is more than can be said for you two, always carping on about conspiracy theories and damn conflicts of interest. And, of course Fuzzy are a great and caring company. We can all benefit from their funding. You agree don't you Enid? Come on tell them what you think about Fuzzy.

ENID: (*starts to cry*) Well they have given me more budget for food, and I will go to national meetings, but,... (*pause*)

CAROLINE: Thats good Enid, see what I mean....

ARCHIE: Let her finish Caroline. Go on Enid. "But" what? What else do you want to say?

ENID: Well, it's just I hate all this arguing, all this bad feeling, I wish people could just get along and I wish as well that I understood things more. When I had an advocate they helped me a lot, but Fuzzy don't think its good to have one anymore.

CHARLIE: Quelle Surprise!

ACT THREE, SCENE EIGHT –

Same old meeting room, two months later, the ex-theatre space in the community centre has been cleared out it is an empty room.

MATT: OK everyone, let's get down to it.

CHARLIE: Hold on Matt, with all due respect, James is chair still, I think, so *he* should call us to order

JAMES: I am leaving it to Matt, everyone, I am not feeling too good, and I don't want another episode like before.

CHARLIE: Well in that case I suggest that I take the chair for the rest of this meeting. Just for form's sake. Everyone agreed? (*everyone nods*) So if I can ask Matt to once again - in simple terms of course - tell us the precise deal with Fuzzy. Unless there are any questions of course. (*pause as he looks around the room*). What? ***No one*** has any questions?

CAROLINE: Well it seems like no one has any doubts now, so Matt you can proceed.

ARCHIE: Just a minute. (*shyly)* I feel like I should know more about the situation, but as I am new I don't feel so bad.

CAROLINE: Oh don't worry dear, everything is pretty self explanatory and all safe and secure for the charity. Believe me everything has been very thoroughly done and all explained to me anyway.

ARCHIE: So just to clarify: you believe in Matt first and foremost

CAROLINE: Yes of course!

ARCHIE: Why? He is new, or so I understand it. On what do you base your trust in him?

CAROLINE: Well I do pride myself on my ability to suss people out and to judge their character. I knew as soon as I met you that you were a trustworthy sort. I could tell you were honest and dependable

ARCHIE: What like Matt you mean?

CAROLINE: Yes exactly!

ARCHIE: But what do you know about me that I didn't tell you?

CAROLINE: Well.... nothing actually, but I trust you.

ARCHIE: Why? The Charity rules clearly state that pleading ignorance is not a valid excuse for any illegality, if you could have found out more about the persons' implicated in wrong doing.

CAROLINE: Well it isn't just about Matt here. Fuzzy are a well respected corporation who support millions through their medications and advice lines.

ARCHIE: Did you know that Fuzzy have just been fined over 3 billion dollars for fraud? They have been paying off thousands of doctors in order to get their meds sold above anyone else's and they have been making fraudulent claims for certain medications, claims which do not fall under the governing body's mandate and certification.

CAROLINE: Oh, so that's why I found you talking to Susan and Charlie. They have been telling you all sorts of stuff I bet.

ARCHIE: Actually no they haven't I found this out for myself because I make it my business to know what I am getting involved in.

CAROLINE: I thought you were on our side, after our talk earlier. But, I find you are a turncoat.

ARCHIE: You assumed I was on your side because, you stupid woman, you have the arrogance and the ignorance to believe what you want to believe.

CAROLINE: Well *really*.! I obviously have read you totally wrongly

ARCHIE: Yes, you have, because as Susan said earlier you do not look beyond the end of your nose which is firmly in the trough of self-protection.

SUSAN: Ha! I like your turn of phrase, Archie.

ARCHIE: Thanks. I told you earlier that you would know if I was being combative.... well this is just the beginning.

SUSAN: Oh Great man!

CAROLINE: Charlie, are you going to do something about this? He is here under false pretenses. He made it quite clear to me before that he was in favour of this way forward.

ARCHIE: If you look back Caroline, I did not *ever* say I was in favour of Fuzzy's funding the project. I simply didn't make my position definitively clear.

MATT: Anyway Charlie, can we move on. So what if Caroline made a mistake on this occasion.?We all allowed to make mistakes once in a while, surely. Don't worry Caroline, everything is going to be OK.

CHARLIE: Have you finished Archie?

ARCHIE: I have barely begun.

MATT: Oh no, are you gonna allow this Charlie?

CHARLIE: As chair and in spirit of fairness, yes I am. Go ahead Archie.

ARCHIE: Thanks, so, Matt, can you tell us just how many charities Fuzzy are now funding and how many are currently in the pipeline?

MATT: I am not privy to that information. I am not high up enough in Fuzzy to be in the know. I am a junior.

ARCHIE: Oh come now don't be shy, tell everyone about who you really are, maybe who your grandfather was, how many shares you have in Fuzzy.

MATT: My private income has no bearing on the deal on the table. I am an employee of Fuzzy yes, but that is all above board. I am just fresh out of college.

ARCHIE: And, yes you are being groomed for a great future.

CAROLINE: Is this true Matt?

MATT: Yes it is, my poor deluded woman. So what if my grandfather co-founded the company? It doesn't make any difference to the Fuzzy funding. They are separate issues.

CAROLINE: James did you know all this?

JAMES: Oh do shut up you self-opinionated bitch. If only you'd kept your mouth shut and kept her mouth shut too, we wouldn't be having this discussion. Anyway it doesn't matter. We have gone beyond the point of no return. We cannot get out of it, the signing is a formality, Matt and I signed three weeks ago to set the whole process in motion. There is no stopping it now, even if we wanted to. Eh Matt?

ARCHIE: Very sure of yourself aren't you James. I see you needed some calming earlier. You've got a ready supply now though haven't you? Why don't you tell everyone what you get out of this deal? No? Cat got ya tongue? Oh look! Here is my dictation device, so let me remind you..... *'Well between you and me I do have a bit of an anxiety problem and I was before all this kicked off, buying Fuzzy anti-depressants and treatment resistant drugs from them online, but now I have a guaranteed supply for life.'* Does that ring any bells?

JAMES: You rat! Who the hell are you?

ARCHIE: Wouldn't you like to know?

MATT: You're a reporter I'd say. Well you've nothing on me. So what if I am a shareholder and my gramps was fortunate enough to co-own the company peddling potions to the grateful and vacuous masses. None of that is a crime. More fool them, the morons and cretins. It is so easy to pull the wool over their eyes. Pinter was right Charlie, we've got the masses where we want 'em, lying back begging for more of everything, But, no one can prove any illegality here.

ARCHIE: Really? Are you sure of that? I have here a dossier of leaked documents gathered over the last five years by me and my team. This proves beyond doubt that you are swindling charities into being drug pushers on a grand scale and infiltrating management committees with your supporters to ensure the regular flow of drug users, defrauding organisations through misrepresentations and by preying on vulnerable people. See James, what you have walked into all because you thought you were right in self-prescribing dangerous addictive drugs.

(Silence)

JAMES: Is this true Matt?

MATT: Of course not. He has no real proof, just some leaked documents. They'll never stand up in court. I suppose you think you'll go to the papers with this? Who knows - maybe you will even write it up for yourself, give yourself some credit. Why not? We all want a piece of the action. You can be bought like the rest of 'em. Even this lot were bought in various ways. Even you two, look at ya! Where did all your research get ya? Eh? No, pipped at the post by a hack. You're pathetic. None of you can touch me and you're tied into the funding process now.

JAMES: Listen you weasel (*taking the signed dossier out of his briefcase)* I don't know anything about your pathetic little contract (*ripping up the contract*) Enid empty that salad bowl and bring it here. No just throw the salad away, there won't be any celebration today. Susan and Charlie I am very very sorry. (*he empties ripped up contract into the bowl and lights with a match*)

MATT: That doesn't signify we have signed copies at head office. The deal stands.

ARCHIE: I am afraid that is not exactly true. You see I am not a reporter, and you're not immune. The paper and computer contents at your head office were impounded two hours ago. Matthew Brinkleman, I am arresting you on suspicion of fraud and deception. You do not have to say anything but it may harm your defence if you do not answer a question which is something you later rely on in court. Anything you do say may be given in evidence.

MATT: What?

EVERYONE: MY GOD!!!!

ENID: What's happening? I need a drink. Anyone else for a fizzy sugary drink? My mum swore by 'em for shock……

CURTAIN

www.ingramcontent.com/pod-product-compliance
Ingram Content Group UK Ltd.
Pitfield, Milton Keynes, MK11 3LW, UK
UKHW020126250726
13967UKWH00002B/502

9 781291 076004